A LEGACY OF ASHES

Z.R. McCORMICK

AN OATHSWORN CHRONICLES NOVELLA

A LEGACY OF ASHES

Z.R. McCORMICK

HILLMARCH
PRESS

A Legacy of Ashes
An Oathsworn Chronicles Novella
By Z.R. McCormick

Published by Hillmarch Press
HillmarchPress.com

ISBN 978-1-966180-09-8 (ebook), ISBN 978-1-966180-10-4 (paperback), ISBN 978-1-966180-11-1 (hardcover), ISBN 978-1-966180-12-8 (jacketed hardcover)

Cover design by Rachel St. Clair

Map design by Z.R. McCormick

For Josh—
We may not have had the streets of Caroca
growing up, but we had our share of adventures
At least some of the neighbors' planters survived.

CONTENTS

Map of Edros … X

Author's Note … XII

1. Price of Survival … 1

2. Fooled … 8

3. Change of Plans … 18

4. Shadows and Kings … 24

5. Choices … 35

6. Legacy … 40

7. The Ashguard … 51

8. Plans … 58

9. Training … 67

10. A Fond Farewell … 81

11. Gilded Shadows … 89

12. The Boy … 97

13. Hunting Rumors … 108

14. The Request … 119

15. Secrets   128

16. Out of Time   142

17. Trapped   152

18. Sacrifice   164

Epilogue   177

Thank You   181

Acknowledgments   183

The Aldarian Compendium   185

Also by   191

About the Author   192

THE ANDERFALLS
KARTHMOOR
STARKHAVEN
KARTHPORT
OAKWAVE
TERESTIA
HARGLOW
DRAGONTAIL
ALJARDIN
MOUNTAI
ARAPHON
NARIQ
ARLINSTAND
BARAND'S LANDING
WESTROCK
PELL
EVERTON
WESTBAY
PELNO
TURIM
THE
GREAT CONTINENT
OF EDROS

FELLINOR
BIRNPASS KEEP
FARGOST
CERN
ALSALAAM
GLASINIR
ISTWYNEIR
MALGAVORN
HAMIDIA
THE LOST HAVENS
RAVEN'S WATCH
AGONAR
MINDEN
VRALN
DORET
LYNREST
ILAGRON
SHEARPOINT MOUNTAINS
ORDA
NEBOA
CAROCA

Author's Note

As it's one of my most beloved stories, I'm so glad you're here to experience Esta's tale! I hope it's as thrilling for you to read as it was for me to write.

Whether you've followed *The Oathsworn Chronicles* from the beginning or are just starting out, you can read *A Legacy of Ashes* as a standalone book as it has no direct connection to the others in the series. However, it does have an ideal spot in the reading order if you enjoy those little "aha" moments. If you'd like to explore more, I've provided my suggested order below to help.

Reading Order for *The Oathsworn Chronicles*
The Cataclysm - a prequel novella
The Chase - a prequel short story
Awakening - Book One
Arrival - a companion short story
Heir - a companion short story
A Legacy of Ashes - a companion novella
The Mages' Merchant - a companion short story coming late 2026
Well of Souls - Book Two coming late 2026

A LEGACY OF ASHES

Chapter 1
Price of Survival

511 GR, 361 Years After The Cataclysm

THE EVENING BREEZE RUSTLED the hem of her silken dress as they left the wide thoroughfare and turned towards the estate's gates. Esta shivered, rubbing the backs of her bare arms. She hated the dress. Hated the way she felt so exposed in its delicate, close-fitting fabric. Really, she would've hated it regardless, simply on principle. Who knew what Rivan had spent acquiring it? Certainly more than they could afford, assuming he hadn't risked stealing it. She scowled at her oblivious brother as he shoved long, black hair out of his face and straightened his patched tunic. It wouldn't matter how hard he tried. Rivan would still stick out like a street beggar entering a noble's feast. Because that's precisely what it was.

"Okay, deep breath," said Rivan as they stopped in front of the high walls of light brown stone and elegant iron gates. He glanced at Esta, studying her from head to toe. "Es, fix that strand of your hair. And make sure that necklace is on straight. I couldn't get real gold, but I think it polished up well enough."

Esta pursed her lips, resisting the urge to put her hands on her hips. It wouldn't do to appear unladylike now. "Seriously? Do I look like I'm twelve still?"

Iron boots clacked on the pavement inside the courtyard, drawing nearer.

"Come *on*," he hissed.

Esta grumbled, detangling the strand of black hair running to her shoulder. It didn't matter that she was officially an adult now. Rivan still treated her like a child anytime he was nervous. The high gate groaned, opening inward as a guard stepped out into the flickering light of the sconces. The Ordan insignia—a phoenix spread before a rising sun—gleamed on his polished chest plate. Esta froze, the same instinct kicking in that she felt every time a guard appeared. The one telling her to run.

"The lord's occupied with his guests tonight. No admittance," said the man irritably, narrowing his brows at Rivan from under his steel helm. "Move on, street rat."

Rivan shook his head, trying to appear collected. "Apologies, sir. You see, we're here by invitation of Lord Gann. Our presence was requested." Rivan pulled a partially crumpled paper from his pocket. The guard snatched it from his hand, scowling as he read. After a moment, he turned the glare back at Rivan, then lingered on Esta.

"Hmph. So, you're another of his special guests, then. Follow me."

The guard motioned them into the courtyard, shutting the gate with a firm click. Esta shivered, this time not from the cold, but from that same feeling. Like being trapped with no escape.

They followed his clinking armor across the paved tiles dividing the immaculate lawn. Ornamental shrubs and broad-leafed palms rustled in the air, their shadows twisting beneath the glowing moon. She couldn't see anything above the walls but the tops of Caroca's other extravagant estates and the starry sky. As hard as life was beyond these walls, what she wouldn't give to be back on the city's dusty streets in the blazing heat of day right now. Rivan nudged her, and she snapped her attention forward. The guard marched up the wide stairs to the estate doors, tugging open their engraved timbers and motioning them inside.

Esta blinked as blinding light and deafening noise slammed into her. A hundred of Orda's nobility filled the expansive hall, mingling, laughing, and feasting. Music rang over the assembly from the corner. Sharp notes from strange, flute-like instruments, for which Esta had no name, and drums of every shape and size echoed off the high, curving ceilings and painted tiles. A dozen scents washed over her. Roasted meat, grilled vegetables, the delicious sweetness of baked treats. Her stomach rumbled, and she forced her hands to remain at her sides. When had she last eaten? She shook away the longing, striding after Rivan and the guard before anyone noticed.

The man in Ordan armor led them through the crowd. Raucous laughter and the din of conversation pummeled her senses, along with the pungent smell of wine on each noble she passed too closely. The tan skin of her arms prickled as several noblemen stared at her. The way they looked at her, that half-masked, shameless hunger, made her insides squirm. She was ready to punch the first one to touch her.

"Breathe," Rivan whispered.

"What?" Her hazel eyes widened as she stole a glance at him.

"Es, breathe."

He was right. She'd been holding her breath almost from the moment they entered the crowd. She let out a shaky sigh.

They crossed the room, exiting into a narrower passage. The guard appeared to take no notice of them as he led on. Chandeliers of hammered bronze and flickering candles lit the hallway from high above them, casting shadows into the other hallways branching off as they passed. The tan, stone walls were impeccably cut, as perfect as everything else she saw. Gann's estate was the most exquisite she had ever seen. Esta took a deep breath as murmurs echoed from farther down the corridor. The guard hadn't been wrong about street rats. She'd never felt so out of place in her life.

The guard stopped beside a large, open doorway, light from beyond reflecting off his armor. He gestured them inside. Rivan led the way, straightening his tunic again as Esta set her gaze in front of her, ignoring the man's pretentious glare.

"Ah, welcome!"

Esta gaped at the sight of the room. A chandelier blazed above her on the curved, plastered ceiling, bathing the polished tile floor and walls in warm light. Short, vibrant palms sat in glazed pots in the corners. Rich, amber-dyed curtains hung over the open windows to unseen courtyards, matching the plush cushions of carved seats and divans along the sides. An array of noblemen sprawled across them, laughing in between sips of their wine. Their robes were of every hue, sewn with bright, precious fabrics and embellishments. The beautiful jewelry adorning their hands nearly left her speechless. The gems on a single ring would have fed her and her brother for months.

Her eyes came to a stop on the man whose voice she'd heard. A thin band of gold pressed into his receding gray hair. His expansive stomach shifted under a costly green and ebony robe, bulging around the golden belt suffocated by his girth. A wide smile gleamed on his pale, pudgy face. He rolled off his side from where he relaxed on his divan, straightening to look at them more clearly.

Rivan took a step forward, bowing low. "Lord Gann."

"I was beginning to wonder if you would make it to our little gathering," said Lord Gann, flashing his repulsive teeth. "Jovan, was it?"

"Jevin, sir."

Esta raised an eyebrow at his false name.

Gann's leisurely gaze slid towards Esta, his eyes suddenly gleaming. "And this lovely woman?"

"Ralla, my lord. My sister."

"Ah, delightful," said Lord Gann, leaning forward. "Your letter spoke the truth. As beautiful as the rare desert blossom, and dressed to match. Wouldn't you agree, my friends?"

The other men chuckled, murmuring in assent.

Esta felt the color rising in her cheeks, her fingers trembling against her pale, silken dress as she pushed away her displeasure. "I... Thank you, my lord." She curtsied stiffly. Lord Gann waved a hand, and the guard approached him. "We are honored to—" Esta froze.

Coins clinked as the guard dropped a heavy cloth pouch into Rivan's outstretched hand. Rivan lowered it to his side, his sheepish face meeting her look of confusion. Suddenly, the guard's gauntleted hands wrapped around her arms, icy metal clamping over her bare skin.

"Wha—Let go of me!" She twisted, but his hold only tightened.

Lord Gann cleared his throat. "My dear, this will be much more agreeable to us all if you would refrain from struggling. It is unbecoming."

Esta paused from her flailing, her perfect hair now hanging wildly across her face. She snapped towards Rivan, seething. "You, you selfish *snake*!"

Her brother shrank back, clutching the pouch closer to his chest.

"Now then, you mustn't blame Jovan," said Lord Gann with a disdainful tone, rising from his seat. "As I understand it, you two have fallen on rather trying times. I expect one must make particularly difficult decisions under such circumstances. And he has made, I believe, a rather beneficial choice for you both."

Esta pulled again at the man's iron grasp, stomping at his steel boots with her sandals. Lord Gann sauntered over to Rivan, patting his shoulder like a comforting friend.

"You must see, my dear. It is simply the price of survival. This way, he has enough to eat, and you, if you behave, will have a whole new life of comfort. I should think that rather exciting!" Lord Gann stepped closer as she ignored the pain and continued fighting against her captor. He bent to her level, meeting Esta's furious glare. The sickening smell of wine hung over him. "It is, after all, only sensible. Surely you understand." Esta stared at him, fuming.

Lord Gann stood back, nodding to the guard. "Please escort our beautiful guest to her new chambers. I will call on her after I have seen to the others." Esta sucked in a breath as the guard forced her to turn. "Oh, and see that she freshens up. A bath would do nicely for her."

"Wait," said Rivan in a small voice. The guard paused as Lord Gann glanced at him in annoyance. Esta shot him a murderous look.

Her brother stepped closer, cautiously extending his arms as the guard held her out. If her mouth had been open, Esta would've let her jaw drop to the floor.

"I'm sorry." Rivan wrapped her in a hug, putting his face next to her ear for the slightest of moments, and whispered, "One hour."

As he pulled away, Esta finally wrenched her arm free of the guard and swung. The slap sent an audible gasp across the room. Rivan held a hand to his cheek, gaping, then darted from the room. The guard seized her arm again—tighter—and pushed her towards the door.

"Well. Rather unsporting to dear Jovan," she heard Gann mutter to the others. "She is fiery, isn't she? A desert blossom, indeed. But after all, it *is* rather sensible, wouldn't you agree?"

Esta howled in rage as the guard and his steely grip forced her on, stumbling down the hall.

Chapter 2
Fooled

THE GUARD YANKED OPEN the solid door, shoving her through it. Esta tripped, catching herself before she nearly collided with a low sofa in the center of the brightly lit bedroom. She swerved towards the door, her breaths coming in ragged huffs. The guard glared at her in return.

"You heard the lord. Over there." He pointed his gauntleted finger at a doorway covered by a thin curtain. "Undress and bathe. He'll be back to enjoy your company soon."

Esta took a step closer, balling her fists. The man frowned. "Don't even think about it. Try to get out and you'll find yourself in the dungeon. They won't be nearly so nice to you there."

He slammed the door, the force reverberating in the small space. A low click emanated from the latch. Esta marched to the door. No matter how she tugged at the handle, it refused to budge. After a moment, the guard's steel boots faded down the hall. She spun around.

Much like his sitting room, it seemed Lord Gann had spared no expense. Another warm chandelier hung from the ceiling, illuminating the brown brick walls and luxurious furniture. A deep, crimson rug covered most of the tile floor, stretching to the wide, plush bed on the far side. Even the bronze bars crisscrossing the windows were made to look extravagant. To Esta, it made, as Gann would likely say, a rather lovely gilded cage. She glanced over at the curtain to the washroom and sighed.

"It's almost a pity I have to leave you. What I wouldn't give for a decent bath."

Esta slipped her hand inside the slit down the side of her silken dress. Carefully, she followed the seam until her fingers found the thin metal strips sewn into it. She carefully slid the lock picks out of the fabric. Then she stepped back to the door, pulling her dark hair behind her ear to listen against the wood for several moments.

Nothing.

Satisfied, she took a deep breath and bent down beside the handle, threading a pick into the lock opening. After a moment of teasing the pick, the lock gave a soft click. Esta grinned. She stood, straightened her dress, and turned the handle.

The hall was still. She could hear nothing, save the faint breeze rustling through the window of her room.

Esta paused, retracing the route the guard had taken from Gann's sitting room. She turned to face its direction and then glanced to her right. It would be that way. Without a sound, she stuffed the picks into her hair behind her ear, and crept down the hall.

She passed a dozen passages and doorways, always pausing before each opening, wary of whoever else might be roaming this quarter of the estate. Time seemed to drag by as she crept deeper into the estate. *I have to be close by now,* she thought.

After another turn, the hall widened at another doorway, more intricate sconces flickering against the polished metal inlaid in the door. This had to be it. She snuck towards the door and gently pulled the handle. It inched open with just a small squeak, but enough to make her jump in the silence. With a nervous glance, she slipped into the room.

Esta exhaled softly. "And here I thought the rest of your place was lavish."

Gilded sconces lined the room, glinting off the water in a small fountain tumbling gently from a lion's face carved into the stone wall. More luxurious sofas and green palms lined the edges. Beyond the far archway, a massive bed sat in the center of a circular bedroom. Its walls were covered with an array of expensive-looking pottery, ancient tools, and decorative daggers atop shelving with sculptures spaced between amber curtains. Esta stepped into the bedroom. A carved desk sat to her left, perfectly built into an alcove in the room.

"There we go."

She strode to the desk, opening each of its wooden doors and shoving aside stacks of paper and inkwells. As she opened one of the larger panels near the bottom, light from the chandelier caught the gleam of metal behind a messy pile of parchments. With a satisfied huff, she shoved them out of the opening, revealing a small safe built into the back of the cabinet. She pulled a pick from her hair and carefully inserted it into the lock. After several attempts, the metal snapped. Esta cursed under her breath, shoving another pick into the slot. With slower movements, she worked again, her heart beating faster with each passing moment. *Come on.*

A muted click emanated from the safe. She sighed. "Yes!"

She swung open the tiny door and reached inside. Her hand brushed against a heavy cloth and pulled out a pouch similar to the one Rivan had received. She teased it open, her eyes brightening as gold and several gemstones gleamed in the light. It was an unexpected bonus, but not why she was here. She sat it beside her and reached deeper into the safe, pushing aside more papers.

It had to be here. They said it was here. Unless... What if they were wrong this time?

Esta swallowed, straining her hand against the cold metal. Her breath nearly caught as more soft fabric replaced the steel.

Another pouch.

Quickly, she pulled it out, bringing the dark, silk bag to her lap. She pulled open its golden strings and reached inside. She felt the coolness of metal and raised it from the bag.

A ring.

Its solid gold shone against the cloth, but it was nothing compared to the fascinating gem set into its top. It was unlike any gem or crystal she had ever seen. A soft, silvery blue stone that seemed to give off its own faint light.

She shook off her trance and turned over the ring, her heart racing. *Where's the marking?*

There.

Engraved in the band of the ring rested the small image of a wolf's head, its eyes locked on Esta. She almost glared back at it.

The Hamid Empire.

A door slammed somewhere down the hall, and she jumped. It was time to leave. Now.

Esta clambered to her feet, shoving the ring and its silk bag into the larger pouch of gold and gemstones. Then she hurried towards the exit.

Creak.

Her heart stopped as the door swung open. There stood Lord Gann, gaping at her as she gaped back. He shook the startled look from his chubby face.

"Well, now. You are quite resourceful, aren't you, my dear?"

Esta gritted her teeth, pulling the pouch behind her. Lord Gann stepped closer, eyeing her with a gleam.

"Sometimes, one can find it difficult to settle in here. It is always a pity when they try to flee. The consequences are rather... unpleasant." He grinned, a hunger whispering behind his repulsive gaze. "However, I cannot say anyone has ever been found waiting in *my* quarters. You are a lovely change of pace." Esta shuffled back towards the wall as he moved nearer, his teeth gleaming.

"Get. Back," she growled.

Gann's smile shifted into a sneer, his gaze sweeping over her body. "You'll find life here rather enjoyable if you embrace it, my desert blossom. Why—" He faltered as he peered at Esta's waist. His eyes flicked towards the desk, widening. She pulled the pouch closer to her back, her heart pounding in her chest. Slowly, he turned back to her, his pointed stare boring into her.

"What do you have in your hands, my dear?"

Esta bumped against the wall, the displays wobbling on the shelving.

Instinctively, she grabbed the handle of a broken awl from its stand with her free hand and threw.

Gann ducked, the relic sailing past him, then he lunged. Esta yelped as his weight crashed into her, ramming her against the shelving and sending a cascade of pottery and displays crashing to the floor. She jabbed her elbow into his neck, and Gann stumbled, losing hold. Esta grasped the rim of a small pot teetering on a surviving shelf and slammed it into Gann's stomach. The clay shattered with a deafening crash onto the tile as he staggered back. Esta sprinted for the exit.

A fat, powerful hand yanked her arm, pulling her to the ground. Esta screamed as the pouch went sailing towards the door. Pain raced across her scalp as Gann pinned her hair against the floor, his sickening breath hot against her cheek.

"Not so fast, my desert blossom. We aren't done here." Esta scowled at him through the tears in her eyes as his face turned to the door. He glanced towards the door, and she looked down. A silent scream rose in her throat.

The ring.

"Tsk, tsk. Well, I must say, that *is* rather unfortunate, my dear. We can't have that particular secret leaving this room now, can we? A pity. I was looking forward to your time with me." He leaned his putrid face back over her. "But it looks like you won't be leaving either."

Esta groped for something, anything, tears burning.

Her fingers brushed an object. She wrenched it from the floor, driving it at his chest. Gann grunted, wobbling back, and the pain in her scalp vanished.

Esta scrambled to her feet, panting for air. She spun towards Gann, fists raised. His considerable body lay sprawled on the floor as he groaned. His round hand clutched at his stomach, blood oozing around a silver dagger embedded in his marred robe.

"You," he hissed. "You will never—"

Esta twirled around, swiping the ring and pouch from the floor as she sprinted for the hall.

Her dark hair flapped wildly around her face as she ran, her stupid dress protesting every step. She had to escape. Which way was she supposed to go again? She rubbed the tears from her eyes. *Think. Think. Gann's room is on the north wall. It faces north. That means I have to go left.* She silently fumed at Rivan. Why in Aldaria had she let *him* pick the spot?

She bolted down the hall, no longer caring if someone heard. The balcony was all she needed.

"Find her!"

Voices echoed from the corridor on her right, and she quickened her pace.

Another turn. Esta raced down the tiled hall, barely registering the others as she sped past.

Snap.

Esta yelped, pain erupting in her shin as she collided with the floor and more of her dress tore. She glanced at her feet and growled, ripping off the broken sandal and the other. *Stupid dress. Stupid shoes,* she fumed, clambering to her feet. *Next time, Rivan gets to wear them.*

She sped down the hall.

Ahead, another, wider hall intersected hers, and beyond it... She nearly leapt for joy.

The starry sky. The balcony.

Her bare feet pounded against the tile, racing for freedom.

Clang.

Boots clacked against the floor, and Esta collided with a metal arm at full speed. The force nearly stole the air from her lungs as the arm slammed her back against the wall.

"Thought you fooled us all, didn't you?" said the guard, sneering. "Your little stunt ends here."

Esta winced as his armored forearm dug into her neck. She clawed at it, pain spreading across her chest. He was too strong.

Fury shone in his eyes. She struggled for air, terrified he meant to strangle her right there.

She lifted her knees, vision flickering, and planted her feet in his chest. The man grunted, and the weight on her throat vanished. She toppled to the floor, head spinning, as the guard fell with a crash. He scrabbled for the blade strapped to his side.

Esta jumped to her feet, still gasping, and ran.

"Stop her!"

Nothing mattered but the stars and sky in front of her, closer with each step, each painful breath. *If there's a god up there, please let Rivan be here.*

She raced onto the balcony, feeling the cool breeze wash over her skin. She scanned the stone railing and sighed in relief.

A metal hook gleamed near the edge, with a rope trailing into the dark.

More boots clattered down the hall.

Without another look, Esta swung herself over the edge, grabbed the rope, and slid from the balcony.

She didn't care how her hands burned. All she wanted was the freedom of dirt beneath her bare feet. Instead, cool, dewy grass met them as she staggered back.

"Esta!" Rivan's voice rang in the silent gloom.

"Here," she said, panting. "Go, go!"

They tore across the lawn and into a grove of trees at its edge as shouts echoed from the balcony.

They didn't stop until they had escaped the upper district, bolted through half the lower district, and reached the crumbling rooftops of the outer slums. By then, Esta could run no more. She stumbled to a halt on the cracked, clay roof tiles of an abandoned storefront. From here, the decadent palaces of Caroca were but a distant gleam, rising over the darkened streets, where sensible people slept. She dropped onto the angled roof, sucking in air as if her life depended on it. She shifted to tuck her legs beneath her, and her fraying dress caught on a piece of broken clay.

Esta cursed under her breath. "Stupid dress."

Rivan flopped down beside her, dangling his legs off the edge of the building. He leaned back on his arms, panting hard, and looked her over. Even in the fading moonlight, she could feel the concern radiating from him.

"Where *were* you?" he said. "We agreed. One hour!"

Esta scowled at him, pushing unkempt hair out of her face. "It took longer than I thought to find it. And I ran into some trouble."

"Trouble? What trouble? Don't tell me that fat noble—"

"Stop. Just..." Esta shivered, pushing horrid thoughts of Gann from her mind. "I took care of him. I got out. That's all that matters."

Rivan pulled his legs back up and faced her. "Did you kill him?"

She shook her head, still trembling. "No. I don't think so. But we'd better lie low for a while."

"Then... Did you get it?"

Esta shot him an irritated look. "Seriously? I nearly died in there, and *that's* what you ask?"

Rivan shrugged. "You just said that's all—"

"Yeah, okay. Here you go." She tossed the jingling pouch at him. Rivan carefully pulled open the silk bag inside, revealing the strange ring.

"Huh," said Esta.

He glanced at her. "What?"

"It really does glow. I wasn't sure when I was inside, but you can definitely see it out here."

They gazed at the mysterious ring and the silvery glow in Rivan's palm. Then he stuffed it back inside its bag. "We'll be rid of it tomorrow. Then we'll feast like kings."

Rivan stood and stretched, offering a hand to Esta.

"What'd you do with the money you got from Gann?" she asked, steadying her shaky legs.

"I've got it here."

Esta folded her arms, frowning. "And how much of it did you spend already?"

Even in the dark, she saw him raise his eyebrows innocently. "What are you talking about? Spend it? Me?"

She rolled her eyes.

"Okay," he said, raising his hands. "Just a little. I had to do *something* to kill time while I waited. Besides, you slapped me."

"You deserved it."

"I did not!" Rivan stomped towards the edge of the roof.

"Oh, yes, you did. You made me wear a stupid dress that nearly killed me!"

Rivan crouched, gauging the distance to the next roof. "You looked nice in it, Es, and you needed to look irresistible. I'd say it worked, right?"

She sighed. "Alright, you win."

He glanced at her, grinning. "I know. It is, after all, rather sensible. Wouldn't you agree?"

"You better jump before I push you."

Rivan laughed and leapt into the dark.

CHAPTER 3
CHANGE OF PLANS

Esta stood in the darkest corner of the alley, biting her lip. At least it was cooler here. She peeked past the cracked plaster of the storefront next to her, watching as another group of rough-looking men staggered out of the midday heat and into the tired tavern. She rolled her eyes, resisting the urge to barge over to the door. *What in Aldaria is taking him so long?*

"Okay, we're clear."

She flinched, nearly smacking Rivan with her fist as she spun around.

"Whoa! A little jumpy today, sis?"

Esta shook her head, pulling at the rough sleeves of her patched shirt. "I'll just feel better once we're rid of this ring."

Rivan raised one of his dark brows. "It's really got you worked up, doesn't it?"

"Rivan. It's from the Hamid Empire. You know, the mages who want to obliterate Orda? Whatever this is all about, it's not good."

"Don't tell me you're superstitious."

Esta put her hands on her hips. "I'm not. I just don't think we should get mixed up with the Empire."

His expression softened as he studied her. "You still blame them, don't you? For our parents."

"You don't?"

Rivan shrugged. "I don't know. I was too young at the time to really understand. One moment they were there, in our wagon of the caravan, and then... they weren't. Just lots of smoke and fire. I know Orda's soldiers never found their bodies."

Esta turned towards the tavern again. She hated revisiting these memories. They didn't help them buy food. Besides, she'd been too little to even remember what flashes Rivan did. "It was them. It wasn't a mistake."

Her brother placed a gentle hand on her shoulder. "Either way, it wasn't fair to us. Wasn't fair to you."

Somehow, his gesture was enough to quell the bitter anger rising in her chest. She turned to face him, pushing down the tide of emotions in her throat. "I, I don't even remember them, Rivan. You at least have their faces, their voices. Me?" She gestured at the alley. "This is all I've got. The slums. A girl who knows more about being a pickpocket and a thief than a daughter."

Pain flickered across Rivan's face. "I..."

Guilt punched Esta in the stomach. "No, I–I'm sorry, that's not what I meant."

Rivan nodded. "You've always got me, Es."

"I know," she whispered. "I'm sorry. You're the one who looked out for me. I survived because of you. And I should be more grateful for that."

Her brother put his arm around her shoulders as she stared at the grimy dirt. His rough fingers found her chin, raising her eyes to his. "We look out for each other, Es. *We* survive together. No matter what."

Esta bit her lip, nodding to keep the tears from falling. She took a deep breath and straightened. "Don't make me cry before we go in there. I'll have to start a bar fight just to stop it."

Rivan laughed. "Save that for another day. Right now, we have some coin to claim."

He strode onto the street with his chin held high. Esta shook her head, then walked out into the light.

The rank smell of sour beer and smelly men invaded Esta's nose as she followed Rivan into the gloomy tavern. The Hog Pen. She wasn't sure if it'd always been that filthy, or if the proprietor had been prophetic. Either way, she couldn't think of a more fitting name.

She trailed closely behind her brother as he wound his way across the packed room, careful to keep away from those she knew had looser hands. Most of the men wouldn't touch her, anyway. She'd scrapped with enough of them by now that they knew what to expect.

"Stayin' out of trouble, little bird?" came a wheezing voice. Esta turned. Old Garrow sat with his mud-stained boots propped on a dirty table, twirling an empty bottle. He wasn't the only one who called her that, but he'd started it. A nod to all the time she'd spent traversing the roofs of Caroca.

"As much as I can."

He flashed her a wrinkled, toothy grin. "Sounds 'bout what I reckon. Long's you fly free. A cage is a terrible place to be."

Esta smiled. "Give me the roofs and sky, and I'll fly."

"That's my girl. One o' these days, ye'll leave this here ground for bigger skies. That's the truth. The slums be too poor for the likes o' you, little bird."

She laughed, though not unkindly. "We'll see." Esta gave him a last nod and hurried over to Rivan, already settling into a table deeper in the shadows. And, thankfully, farther from the stench of the bar.

Esta slowed, noticing another figure there waiting. A woman, dark-skinned, like many of those from the neighboring country of Neboa. Her black hair was shaved close to her head, and dusky leather armor covered her from the neck down. Elowë only knew how many blades she had in all the pockets, pouches, and folds sewn into the leather. Like the others Esta and her brother had worked with, this woman was not someone to take lightly.

"Esta," said Rivan, inclining his head towards the woman. "Ghenda."

Ghenda gave a slight nod, her brown eyes studying Esta. She felt awkward under the older woman's penetrating gaze, as if she knew more about Esta than she did herself.

"Word is, Lord Gann's party went a little sideways," said Ghenda in her deep voice.

Esta nodded and started to speak, but Rivan cut her off. "We did the job, and we've got what was promised."

Ghenda's eyes narrowed, passing between them. "Is it with you?" Rivan reached for his pocket. "No," she growled. He froze.

"No?" said Esta.

Ghenda shook her head once. "Not here. Your job's moved beyond the Guild's involvement."

Rivan's gaze flicked to Esta. She felt the worry in his eyes. Probably as much as he felt hers.

"What do you mean?" he asked.

"The client has requested to meet with you. Directly."

Rivan folded his arms. "That's not how your Guild works. We've never had a job ask that before."

Ghenda shifted in her seat, her expression never wavering. "There are extenuating circumstances for this one. The contract with the Guild is satisfied, as long as you deliver the package to the client."

Rivan sucked in a breath and turned to Esta again. She tilted her head, which told him all he needed to know. It's not like they had a choice. You didn't walk away from a contract with the Thieves' Guild. Not if you wanted to live.

"Alright." He sighed. "Where?"

Ghenda slid a small scrap of parchment to Rivan. "You'll find the client here. They know to expect you." Her brother unfolded the paper. "The Guild would prefer you resolve this matter today. We dislike letting contracts linger."

Esta looked over as Rivan's head shot up, eyes wide. "Th–this is in the upper district. Isn't this...?"

Ghenda frowned. "Deliver the package, and your obligations to the Guild are fulfilled."

Rivan looked like he was about to say more when Esta touched his arm. "We'll take care of it."

The woman nodded slightly, then stood from her chair. Men scooted farther away as she passed, their voices quieting, until the door slammed shut behind her.

Esta glanced back at Rivan, her brother still staring at the paper. "What is it?"

He looked up at her with a hint of dread in his eyes. "Es, this is the king's private gardens. In the upper city."

Fear dropped into her gut like a weight. "That, that can't be right. Maybe you have it wrong."

Rivan pursed his lips. "Seriously? I don't know Caroca?"

"It was worth a try."

He groaned. "What have we gotten ourselves into?"

"I told you it was bad news."

"So, what do we do?"

Esta glanced across the room at the dingy windows, faint daylight filtering through the dirty air. "Looks like we're going to see King Attas."

"You can't be serious."

She shot him her most serious look. "You want to be dead?"

Rivan raised the paper, shaking it at her with a scowl. "I... hate it when you're right. Ugh. Let's get this over with."

Chapter 4
Shadows and Kings

Rivan paced anxiously in the gloom, glancing at the high walls across the street in between every gilded carriage that passed and every pompous crier demanding the lesser people make way for his master. Esta sat atop a stack of crates above him, grinning as one particularly eager dog escaped from its frantic owner and set to chasing a chubby crier farther up the street. *Shows him who's boss.*

"What if they arrest us? Or kill us?" said Rivan. "Sweet Elowë, do you think King Attas still uses the torture chamber?"

Esta rolled her eyes and dropped onto the cracking cobblestones between the shops. "Why in Aldaria would the King of Orda hire us to steal something *from his own noble* if he was only going to torture us? Come on, Rivan. That's ridiculous."

"Maybe it was a test—to see if Gann's defenses were solid—and we weren't supposed to succeed. Or maybe someone planted the ring on him, and we were supposed to get rid of it, but now we're the loose end!"

She stood right in his path with her hands on her hips, forcing him to stop. "You're being paranoid. *Maybe* the Empire bought off Gann, and Attas needed proof. *Maybe* he'll be so thankful we caught a traitor, he'll give us Gann's estate."

Rivan crossed his arms. "Now who's being ridiculous?"

"I can dream, can't I?"

He shook his head.

"Come on," said Esta, turning back to the street and dusting off her tattered pants. "It's no good hiding here. Might as well face it."

She waited for a break in the traffic heading into the heart of the upper district, then marched across the paved street. Esta could feel the whispers and stares following her. She knew what they said, what they thought.

Street rat. Beggar.

Out of place and where she shouldn't be. The slums were her cage. Kept out of sight, where she belonged. She clenched her fists.

A cage was a terrible place to be.

And if this was her moment to stand before the king, the moment this little bird could fly free, she would take it. Condescending nobles be damned. Esta held her chin high and marched towards the gilded gates.

She slowed as she drew closer to them. A verdant forest of emerald, yellow, and even pink carpeted the gardens beyond the gates. A sweet, fragrant scent wafted through the opening, filling her with a longing to race across the soft grass, and to dip her toes in the cool lake she'd heard rumored in its depths. She came to a halt in the shadow of the gardens' lofty walls. Two

Ordan soldiers in golden armor with bright spears stood beside the gates, watching the crowd milling past with unwavering focus.

None came unbidden to the king.

"Es..." Rivan whispered behind her.

She stepped forward.

The moment she parted from the throng, the soldiers' attention snapped to her. She pushed aside the accusations whispering in her head. It didn't matter whether the soldiers saw her like the rest of them or not. She was here because they'd been summoned.

"State your business, citizen," said the first soldier, firm, but not callous.

Esta raised the paper from Ghenda. "My brother and I were asked to deliver something. On behalf of a certain... group. A token from an enemy of the king."

The soldier glanced at the other, both of their faces deadly serious. His dark eyes snapped back to her, so fast she almost flinched.

"You are expected." He gestured through the gates, their golden, weaving bars gliding open without even the slightest sound. "Please follow this path. You will be met along the way."

Esta curtsied, unsure of what else to do, and hurried inside. Rivan shot her an excited look as he matched her pace, the smooth gravel crunching under their ragged shoes. She glanced back, watching as the gates closed behind them. More than a handful of passing nobles and others in the rich garb of the upper class stared after them, the shock plain on their faces. She almost stuck out her tongue. But then, that would be very unladylike. Especially in the king's gardens. So instead, she flashed a sneer and marched on.

Cool shade enveloped them as the stony path wound into the trees. Rivan walked beside her as if lost in a dream, gazing at more varieties of trees than Esta knew existed. Bees buzzed past, busy among the rainbow of flowers, and a multitude of dazzling birds sang in the branches. At that moment, she wanted nothing more than to kick off her dirty shoes and feel the coolness of the earth. To lie in the inviting grass and simply drink in the stillness of life around her. Maybe there really was a lake ahead, and she'd be one of the few souls alive to see it. What if she could even feel it?

Rivan made a noise, and Esta snapped forward. Ahead sat a man on a simple stone bench beside the gravel path, stooped over an open book in his lap. He hadn't appeared to notice them. Esta raised a brow. He looked oddly out of place in an Ordan garden, yet also not, with his relaxed posture.

She'd seen a handful of similar, brown-skinned foreigners in Caroca over the years, usually merchants from far off Araphon in the north. Enough passed through that she'd learned to avoid them, or else risk the insults from other street urchins claiming she too must be an Imperial. Like she'd somehow determined her own darker complexion.

Though most of the merchants she'd seen had kept their thick, black hair longer, this man's was cut short to his skull. He wasn't exactly old, but she guessed probably old enough to have been her father. Even so, his attention never left the unfolded pages. Rivan slowed, moving closer to her as they neared.

The man glanced up, his dark eyes meeting hers over a charming smile. "What's this? More guests of the king arriving today? Well met, friends."

Esta gave a small nod, unsure how to respond to this stranger.

"What errand brings you to the gardens of King Attas?"

"A matter for his ears, I'm afraid," said Rivan, discreetly nudging her on.

"Ah, of course, of course. One can scarcely number the appeals laid upon him these days. All of them pressing, as you'd expect. I'm afraid there is quite a wait for his attention this afternoon." The man gently shut his book and rose to his feet, placing it under his arm as he smoothed the front of his fitted, amber tunic. Its silk threads were expertly woven and unadorned, save for a gold pin on its high collar. A phoenix in flight.

He gestured to the path. "If this is your first time in the gardens, might I suggest a stroll past the water on your way? You won't find the king's queue any worse for waiting."

Esta's hazel eyes gleamed. "So there *is* a lake!"

Rivan's elbow jabbed her side. "Sorry, but we have to go."

"Rivan." Esta glared at him. "You'd really pass on your one chance to explore just a little bit?" He stared at her like she'd slapped him again.

The man chuckled. "It is but a slight detour. You'll see your errand finished just as well by its path. It'd be my pleasure to show you the way."

Esta bit her lip, an inkling of suspicion still nagging at her. But it was her only chance. She'd lost count of the cool, rippling lakes she'd daydreamed of dipping her toes in while wiping dusty sweat from Caroca's arid streets off her brow. In some of them, she'd even learned to swim.

She nodded, doing her best to appear nonchalant rather than bursting with excitement.

"Excellent! If you will, my friends. You will not be disappointed." The man folded his free arm across his chest with a slight bow, then strode down the path. Esta chased after him, ignoring Rivan's sour mood as gravel crunched under his steps.

"So," she said, edging up beside the man. "Who are you?"

"Ah, that's right, forgive me." He inclined his head with a smile. "Medin, a friend of Attas'. And you?"

"Esta. That's my brother, Rivan." She shot Medin a curious look. "A friend? Hard to imagine King Attas having just a regular friend."

Medin laughed. "Is it? I suppose it is for most. All of Orda looks to him for direction, for leadership. The king embodies the strength of his people, you might say. He must, for the threat of the Empire ever looms." His expression sobered. "They forget a king is but a man. Mortal. He feels, just as they do." Medin leaned closer with a grin. "He even stubs his toes."

Esta smirked. "I hate it when I do that."

"Right? Attas is as much flesh and bone as his lowest subject. And just as flawed, as he'd readily admit. But good. To tell you the truth, I think he dislikes the way his nobles and people treat him, as if he's greater than they. He'd rather be seen as you and I—as a person. And not through the gilded cage of his reality."

Esta nearly stopped short. She shouldn't be feeling sorry for a king. He had no idea what a real cage was like. "I'd take a palace over the slums any day."

Medin lifted a dark brow over his knowing eyes. "We often dream of what we don't have. Ever chasing things and pleasures. Attas has it all, and at the end of all things, none of it will go with him. A true king understands. His gaze must be beyond what is under the sun."

Esta frowned, unsure of what to make of it all. Medin was unlike anyone she'd ever met. Likeable, but different.

"Ah!" Medin glanced back at her with an excited look. "Just past these trees." He stopped at a curve in the path, placing his arm across his chest again as he gestured on. Esta glanced at him and turned. Her eyes widened.

A perfectly clear, blue lake stretched in every direction, ringed by forest. Sunlight gleamed off its tranquil waters, the reeds of its shores rustling in the gentle breeze. Suddenly, the heat seemed to press through her stiff, dusty shirt. It took all of Esta's restraint not to dash for its edge and plunge herself in. Medin smirked at her as she gawked, like he knew her mind.

"Come on."

A narrow jetty ran from the shore into the water, with more benches along its edge. Medin led them onto the stony dock, and Esta closed her eyes, savoring the cool breeze tickling her hair and face.

"I suggest bringing your own book the next time you visit," said Medin, settling onto a bench. "You'll find this a rather excellent spot to pass the day."

Esta stepped to the end of the dock, staring at the rich blue swirling beneath her. She could see down to the rocks on its shallow bed. Schools of tiny fish darted through her shadow, disappearing under the dock and reappearing again in the light.

"Do you swim?"

Esta turned to Medin with a scoff. "Swim? In Caroca? You couldn't pay me to even jump in one of its wells."

Medin laughed. "Fair. There's not much chance beyond this old oasis, I suppose. But you can at least dip your toes in."

Rivan frowned from the shore. "Es, we really need to get going."

She ignored him, fixing a serious gaze on Medin's beaming face. "This is the king's gardens. Isn't that breaking the rules? I'd probably get thrown into a cell!"

He stifled another laugh. "I can assure you, there's no rule. You're quite safe."

Esta bit her lip, staring at the water. *Just for a moment.*

She slipped out of her too-small shoes, exhaling as the dock's smooth stone met the bareness of her tired feet. Cautiously, she settled on the edge and lowered her legs.

The water was like a cool, exhilarating world, her callused feet now leagues apart from the baking heat smothering the rest of her. She'd never felt something so wonderful in her life.

Medin took a seat across from her, pulling up the legs of his loose, ashen pants and dipping his own feet in. He looked at her with another infectious grin.

"Can you keep a secret?"

"Yes..." she said, growing suspicious.

Medin's dark eyes gleamed. "I've even pushed Attas in."

Esta shook her head, trying to hide a smile. "You're lying."

"I swear to you. And it doesn't leave this dock. He'd die of embarrassment."

She giggled, turning back to drink in the lake.

Suddenly she froze, staring at the water. *Giggling?* What in Aldaria was she doing? She hadn't giggled like that since she was a child. You didn't giggle in the slums of Caroca. You fought rats for the scraps bakers threw out at night.

Esta frowned, pulling her knees to her chest. "Rivan's right. We need to go."

Medin clicked his tongue. "Attas is fine. The last thing he needs is to worry about the ring today."

In an instant, all of her instincts slammed into reality, sending her heart racing.

"*What* did you say?"

Rivan stomped closer. "We didn't say anything about a ring."

Esta scooted to the very edge of the dock, grasping for her shoes. "Just who are you, really?"

Medin didn't move. He simply gazed out at the still water. "You did well, Esta," he said at last. "I knew you would."

Everything told her to leap to her feet and dash for the exit. But instead, she sat there, glued to the cold stone seeping into her feet.

"You're the client."

"I am."

Rivan stepped between them, his fists tightening. "Why'd you bring us here? What's your game, Medin?"

The man studied Rivan, expressionless. Fear clutched at Esta's chest, her legs trembling. He'd pulled all the right strings. Like he knew exactly how to disarm her. How did he know her so well? She'd *liked* him. It made her sick.

"There's no game, Rivan," he said slowly. "But I needed you to trust me."

"Trust?" Esta nearly choked on the word. "You lured me here and toyed with me. And you expect us to *trust* you?" She stomped to her feet.

Esta jammed her hand into her trousers and ripped the silk bag from her pocket. She tossed it beside him. "There. The job's done. Pay us so we can go."

Medin stared at her. Something in his gaze made her feel, what? Guilty? Was that pity in his eyes? Esta scowled in return. She didn't want his pity. Just his coin.

"There's more going on here, Esta. More you could do to help. Not just to help me or Attas, but all of Orda."

She stretched out her palm.

Medin sighed, placing his hand into the fold of his shirt. When he opened his hand to her again, a single coin rested in the center. Her mouth nearly fell open.

A king's mark.

A massive ruby cut into the likeness of a phoenix gleamed in the center of the large, golden coin. She couldn't move. It was worth more than all the jobs they'd ever pulled. Enough to buy a house near the upper district. Only the king's greatest champions ever received them. Usually as a gift to their family after they'd been killed fighting the Empire. Medin looked at her knowingly.

"You'll be free of the slums, Esta. Free to go where you will and make your own life."

He said exactly what her heart wanted to hear. What she'd dreamed about for years. Only now it rang like a lie. Too smooth. Too calculated.

She snatched the token from his hand and shoved it into her pocket. He chose the wrong words. And she hated him for it.

"Come on, Rivan."

Medin stood as she turned and stomped down the dock, still clutching her shoes in her hand. "You don't want to know what I'm offering?"

"Nope."

She knew it. She knew getting involved in anything with the Empire, with kings... It was a terrible idea.

"Your parents died for this chance, Esta. Don't you want to know why?"

She froze.

Rivan nearly choked as he staggered beside her.

Esta swerved around, hair whipping across her face. "Stop it. You know nothing about me, Medin. Or my parents."

He looked at her with that same pitiful look from before. "Esta, Lara and Davin were the closest family I had. They died for something bigger than themselves. Bigger than all of us."

Their names. How did he know their names?

She shook her head, forcing back the angry tears as she shut her eyes. "You don't know. You couldn't."

"Esta."

She opened them. Medin stood in front of her, tears rolling down his cheeks. "Lara was my sister. Your father was Attas' brother."

Esta stared at him in disbelief.

"I'm your uncle."

CHAPTER 5
CHOICES

Esta rolled the king's mark between her sunburned fingers, watching as the sun sank behind the mountains. The warm, clay tiles beneath her dangling legs were comforting, like an old friend. She gazed across the roofs of Caroca, her eyes drifting towards the king's palace. A tiny speck compared to the mountains' rocky heights behind it.

She was, what? A noble? A princess? It didn't matter, regardless. Attas had his own children, his own family to continue the line of kings. He didn't need them. He didn't even seem to know she and Rivan existed. Wouldn't want more complications in his gilded cage. And she didn't want his titles. He'd given her everything she needed, and it was right here in the palm of her hand.

Except there was Medin.

Her stomach churned, thinking back to the cool waters of the lake. She and Rivan didn't have to fight to survive anymore. They could find a house in the nicer part of Caroca, where Rivan could get a decent job, and she might find a noblewoman willing to teach her everything her mother couldn't. They could escape the slums, and she'd finally be free to fly wherever she wished.

So why did she want to just move into a nicer cage?

Or they could join their uncle. He hadn't simply promised a room in Attas' gilded halls. He'd also promised danger. Something that would send her down the same path as her parents. Something that could end with her joining them.

She huffed. *Some uncle.*

Rivan clambered onto the roof of their hideout, crawling over beside her. His long legs dangled next to hers, his shoulder brushing her own. It was even more comforting than broken roof tiles in the slums.

"You haven't moved for an hour now."

Esta ran the coin through her fingers again. "I know."

"Want to talk?"

She shrugged.

They sat, watching as the light faded and evening's first stars peeked into existence. Gradually, the radiating warmth of the tiles faded, and Esta shivered. Rivan scooted closer.

"Medin will want to know in the morning," he said in a low voice.

Esta made a sound. "I'm sure he'll be busy locking Gann up in a traitor's cell."

"Well. After that. By the way, you were right." She raised a brow at him. "You think that mark will cover Gann's estate?"

She laughed, shoving him lightly. "There isn't a chance in the world I'm going back there. Unless it's to burn it down."

Rivan chuckled. "Guess we need to find a different house, then."

Esta dipped her head, staring at the gleaming coin.

"You don't want to, do you?"

She snapped her gaze back to him. "Of course I do."

He shot her a look. "Seriously?"

Esta crossed her arms, trying to look offended. "What? You think I want to follow Medin off on some harebrained job *in the Empire*? Do I look crazy?"

"Sometimes. Ow!" Rivan rubbed his arm, shoving her fist away. "All I'm saying is, I've been okay with the smaller jobs we've worked in the past. They got us by. But taking the Gann job was *your* idea. You got that excited look in your eye and saw all the coin waiting at the end."

Esta stared at him, fuming. "We needed the money! We were starving, Rivan!"

Pain flashed across Rivan's face. "And what about the danger to *you*? I walked out of that estate and *hated* myself for it. What if I'd lost my sister in that place? I'd rather us be hungry than lose you!"

She flinched. She'd never doubted Rivan's love for her. Honestly, he could be overprotective at the best of times. But looking at him now, she hadn't realized just how deeply her risks could hurt him.

Rivan scooted away, glaring off into the darkness. Esta lowered her head, staring at the shadows in the alley. She shut her eyes and sighed.

"I'm sorry," she whispered. "I didn't think about how it'd make you feel."

He stiffened, then turned again to face her. "It's just... Everything's getting more dangerous, Es. What if the next job doesn't go like we plan?"

"You think I *want* danger?"

Rivan shrugged. "I think you want something more than money and a comfortable life. I just don't know that there's anything under the sun that'll actually satisfy you." Esta looked at him like she'd been hit. He sounded like Medin.

He raised an eyebrow. "What?"

"Nothing." She shook her head, pushing away the nagging feeling in her gut. "I'm not looking for danger, Rivan. I'm not sure that we *should* join him."

Her brother pursed his lips. "You're a terrible liar, Es. That look from the Gann job? You had that same gleam with Medin before we left."

She hid her face behind her hair, her hand digging into the edge of the cracked tiles. Deep down, she knew he was right. It wasn't any wealth or prestige Medin was offering. He definitely wasn't offering that. She wasn't even sure it was the answers about her parents she really wanted.

So why was she drawn to it? Why risk everything for a job and a man she hardly knew? Vengeance? Glory? Esta snorted. *Sweet Elowë.* She was just as lost as the little girl Rivan had pulled away from a burning caravan.

"So, who's going to tell him?"

"Huh?" Esta's head jerked up.

"Medin. You want to let him know we're in, or want me to?"

Her eyes widened. "I—we're not—"

"Es. It's written all over your face." He slid his hand over hers, pulling the king's mark from her grip. He raised it, the ruby gleaming in the growing moonlight. "If we took this and bought that house, you'd spend the next year moping around like the time that sparrow you caught got loose."

Esta huffed. "I would not!"

"You would, too. And we'd both be miserable until you snuck back into those gardens and begged Uncle Medin to take you back."

"I don't beg." She snatched the mark from his hand. "And there isn't a chance in Aldaria I'm calling him 'Uncle' Medin either."

Her brother chuckled. "Sounds a bit strange, doesn't it?"

"Rivan," Esta said, turning serious. "He's talking about infiltrating the Empire. The people who killed our parents. We could end up the same way."

"Yeah, we could." Rivan moved closer, wrapping his warmth around her shoulders. "Or we could finally get answers about what really happened to them and stop the Empire from doing something worse."

She looked up at him, thrill and terror mingling inside her. "Then... you're in? We're really going to do it?"

Rivan nodded. "Either way, Es, we look out for each other. No matter what."

Chapter 6
Legacy

T HEY'D LOOKED A LOT less imposing from the bustle of Caroca's streets.

Esta bit her lip, shifting her feet as she stared up at the towering palace and the gold inlays of its gates. They were even higher than the garden's had been. Somewhere inside, her uncle sat on a throne, deciding the fate of her country's future.

King Attas. Also, her uncle.

Never in a thousand years would that have been one of her dreams. Was she supposed to bow before the king now? How many guards would tackle her to the floor if she tried to hug him? Maybe it was best to start with a curtsy.

"Well?"

Rivan's voice shook her from her anxious thoughts. She turned to look at him, hardly believing the man standing next to her was the same one who pulled their only tattered blanket off her every night while she slept. Rivan tugged at the sleeve of his fitted, navy shirt, messing with the golden clasp at his wrist. His dark pants and polished leather boots complemented his tanned complexion well, and... Esta rolled her eyes.

"Seriously? You're going to see the King of Orda with your hair messed up like that?"

"What?" Rivan ran his hand through his loose, black hair, attempting to pull down its stubborn end.

She sighed. It was probably too much to expect the slums to give up their hold on him in a single day. Maybe by next week.

"You look good, Es," he added, "even if it's not a dress."

Esta smiled. It probably wasn't what women were expected to wear before nobility, but Medin had humored her. The pants and boots were like Rivan's, perfectly snug against her thin legs. But it was the white, cotton shirt she appreciated most. Its soft, loose sleeves and wide neck were utterly simple, but that was the point. It made her feel free. She'd even accepted the golden necklace Medin had given her after he'd waved away the heavy, constricting dress the tailor had brought. She ran her finger across the small sapphire at its end. *Stupid dress*. It made her like her uncle all the more.

"Are you ready?" Rivan asked, glancing at the soldiers in golden armor beside the gates. The men watched them, just as serious as the ones from the gardens.

"Yeah." She looked up at the clouds racing overhead. *If you're up there, please let me get through this without messing something up.*

Rivan stepped towards the gates, and Esta followed.

The guard on her right raised a fist, knocking the wood with a single, firm thump. The massive timbers creaked open. Specks of light from high chandeliers flickered in the gloom as Esta blinked after the brightness of the day.

"Welcome, welcome!"

A short, older man hurried to them with a slight bow. "We have been expecting you both with much anticipation. Please, your uncles are this way, if you will follow me, Master Rivan and Lady Esta."

Lady Esta? She frowned. That was a title she could do without. She sounded like another self-important noble. Rivan shrugged at her, then trailed after the little man. With a last roll of her eyes, Esta followed.

The palace halls were of the same light brown stonework that most of Caroca's estates shared. As were the high ceilings and lavish curtains, billowing about the open windows. But it was the faint, scented breeze that caught her attention, and she paused. Below them, the king's gardens rustled like a sea of green, stretching beside the city in the distance. She longed to be back among its trees by the lake, back in its serenity, even though she *was* eager to meet another of her relatives. It was what would come after that roiled her thoughts.

"If you please, Master Rivan, Lady Esta." The man bowed, holding a thick wooden door ajar.

"Just Esta," she said flatly as Rivan slipped inside.

"Ah, forgive me, but titles are expected among the king's nobility, Lady Esta." His kind, wrinkly face beamed at her, making it hard to glare back. "Even though we are to keep your arrival quiet for the time being, you are an honored part of his household now."

Instead, she pursed her lips, gave a small nod of thanks, and marched into the room.

"Well, we were wondering where you'd gotten off to."

Esta tore her gaze from the towering cases of books lining the stone walls. Light flooded the lofty room from a massive bank of windows overlooking the gardens, making the grand library far more inviting than it would have otherwise been. She'd never seen so many books in her life. Medin sat at a small, carved table below the windows, an open book beside him. Another figure stopped pacing across from her uncle and met her stare.

"King Attas," she said with a gasp. She dropped into a stumbling curtsy as Rivan bowed. The king's face softened, and he waved his hand.

"No, no, Attas will do," he said in a deep voice. "We are family, after all, are we not? I don't expect Medin to bow to me either." He glanced good-naturedly at her other uncle.

Medin smirked. "Well, I am glad we're past that stage."

Although his complexion differed greatly from Medin's, Attas had the same affable presence about him that Esta had sensed upon meeting Medin. The king was older, heavier set, and with peppery hair almost the length of Rivan's. Crow's feet appeared beside his gleaming brown eyes every time he smiled, and as skeptical as she was, Esta couldn't help but admit there was a distinct likability to him.

"Now," he said, clapping his hands. "Let me see my nephew and niece more closely. Come, join us."

The king placed his hands on Rivan's shoulders, studying her brother's face as he approached.

"Yes... So like Davin," he murmured, a flicker of grief in his otherwise joyous expression. "You are certainly my brother's son."

Rivan swallowed. "You—you really knew my father then?"

"Well, I should hope so! Got me into enough trouble, he did. I cannot tell you the number of times we were sentenced to sweeping the stables for his antics."

Esta grinned. Somehow, knowing all the ridiculous things Rivan had done over the years made Attas' claim even more credible.

"And you." The king turned to Esta, and she snapped to attention. "There is much of him in you as well. But a lovelier grace, I must say. That most certainly is Lara. Elowë knows Davin had none."

A lump formed in her throat. "Please, we want to know about them. We want to know what our parents were like."

Rivan stepped to her side, his own face filled with emotion. "And what happened to them. What *really* happened."

Attas nodded solemnly to Medin, his own expression filled with sorrow.

Medin sighed. "Your parents embodied the best of Orda. The best of Aldaria, really. They were a cherished part of our lives. But their union risked everything, and fate couldn't be stalled forever."

The king shook his head, folding his hands behind him as he looked out at the shining lake. "My brother... No. Medin, it's best if you continue."

He nodded. "Your mother's family—my family—is of a lesser house of Araphon. Noble, but not within the high prince's circle in the capital of Aljardin. My family is not of an old wealth like many of theirs, but one we fashioned through our merchants. We fought for status, and took every deal we could, even to Orda. It was my leading of caravans to Caroca that doomed them."

Esta crossed her arms. "You're telling me our mother was an Imperial? That *I* am, and you are?"

"*Was.*" Medin rubbed the back of his neck. "Not that I can change my birth. It's been years since I've set foot outside of Caroca. Too many dangers. Too much old blood.

"Your mother often accompanied me when I traveled to negotiate our contracts. She enjoyed seeing the world." He shook his head. "*And* she was my favorite little sister. It was hard to say no."

"I know what that's like," Rivan muttered. Esta elbowed him with a dirty look.

"It was on one of those trips to Caroca that she met Davin, your father," Medin continued. "My own fault for letting her wander the city while I spun my words."

Attas chuckled. "You make it sound as if Davin were some falcon waiting to swoop down upon her."

Medin shrugged. "Yes, swooping is bad. In their case, however, love came to them quickly. And there was no dissuading Lara once she set her mind to something. It didn't matter that our father threatened to disown her. She wouldn't stay locked away in Alsalaam, chained to a life he made for her."

"She wanted to be free," said Esta quietly.

"You're more like her than you realize," he said, nodding. "Lara chose to run all the way to Orda. For him."

Esta took a deep breath. She couldn't imagine making that kind of choice. Like letting your whole world die for something new. "She must have been terrified."

King Attas turned to her, his expression both gentle and sad. "Lara certainly was when she came to us, but Davin didn't hesitate. They wed within the month, much to our father's displeasure. My brother knew what she had sacrificed, and there was nothing he wouldn't do for her."

"I visited a year after they wed," said Medin. He looked at Rivan. "That's when I first met you. Only a few months old, but it was clear you, and Esta after you, were their entire world."

Rivan scrunched his face like he was struggling for words. "I... I don't remember that."

Esta rolled her eyes. "Did you expect to?"

Medin's face darkened, and he stood, walking away from the group. "That trip. If I could go back and change it all... Maybe none of this would've happened."

"You couldn't have known," said Attas gently. "None of us could have."

Esta's stare bored into Medin as he turned, wracked with guilt.

"Lara. She tried to tell me before I returned to Araphon. I didn't understand what she was saying at the time. Something about an old friend and a house that she'd stopped at as she fled. She—she wasn't making any sense!" He slumped into a chair, putting his head in his palms. Attas took a seat beside him, appearing lost in his own bitter thoughts.

"Lara had a close friend in Ilagron she'd met while at school. Father sent all of us there to the Fountmore Academy when we came of age," Medin continued. "By the time Lara fled Araphon, her friend's brother had gained an estate in southern Hamidia. Lara ended up lost and out of money, begging for safety at his doors. But Elowë was watching over her that night. Her friend happened to be visiting him when Lara stumbled onto its grounds. She found refuge, but her curiosity doomed her and Davin both."

Esta pushed down the dread rising in her stomach. "How?"

"Lara found something inside the estate when she went looking for her friend. Something she shouldn't have seen. She couldn't explain to me what it was, and I was too callous to bother trying to understand. My mind saw only the contracts and trade negotiations waiting for me back in Alsalaam." He hung his head. "Fool. I was a fool."

"It is a miracle she left that place alive. I'm still not sure why this man didn't stop her that night. But it hung like a shadow over them every day after. It wasn't until years later, when soldiers appeared on my doorstep, that I learned the Empire had murdered them."

"They came for you, too?" Rivan asked.

Medin stiffened. "It… is a story best left for another day. But in time, I found my way back to Caroca, searching for the answers Lara tried to give me. Answers I've spent years since chasing. And then, Elowë led me to you."

Esta looked at Rivan. "Us?"

Medin made a noise and scowled. "I was chasing another lead when I stumbled upon Gann's treachery. He had somehow become caught up with others connected to this man from Hamidia, feeding Ordan secrets to the Empire under our very noses."

"You needed to take him out." Esta smirked at Rivan. *I knew I was right.*

Medin nodded. "Gann, however, had many powerful allies in Caroca. Within the palace, too. I couldn't simply send my people into his estate without him realizing we were on to him. I needed outside help."

Rivan shook his head. "The Thieves' Guild."

"Yes. I have my own ways of keeping tabs on the Guild, but I knew they'd be reliable in this instance. What I didn't count on was their sending you. And at first, I tried to stop them."

"Wait." Esta raised her hands. "You knew it was us? That we were Lara's children?"

"Not exactly. Not at first. But the moment I saw you both, accepting the contract from the Guild... Esta, it was like my sister's ghost walked out of that tavern."

"I don't remember seeing you."

"If I'd wanted you to see me, you would have. But your appearance, the both of you together, and your ages... I had to be sure. I needed more information. And so I watched and listened."

"You were following us?" Rivan asked.

"Sometimes." Her uncle shrugged. "But I have eyes in many places. Some with *old* memories. Two little children wandering into the slums of Caroca aren't as easily forgotten as you might think."

"Who...?" Esta stopped. "No way."

He tapped the table beside him with a knowing smile. "He's one of my most reliable informants. A natural."

"Old Garrow? Really?" Esta thought back to all the encounters she'd had with the elderly beggar over the years. It dawned on her that he'd been around more times than she'd realized. Especially as a child.

"You were in excellent hands all the way until you stepped into Gann's estate."

A knot formed in Esta's stomach. "Why'd you let me go? Why send me in?"

Medin frowned, gripping his knees tighter. "I'd learned enough about your past to know the Guild was right to choose you for the job. You both had proven your talent. But only you had the skills and charm to pull it off, Esta. Gann had a weakness, and you played him like a drum."

Rivan scowled at him. "You could've at least warned us. There had to be another way that didn't risk my sister's safety!"

Medin sighed. "Contacting you could've tipped Gann off in any number of ways. And believe me, if I'd found one, Gann would've been in irons before you ever set out that night. But my hands were tied. You were the only ones I could trust. Esta passed the test, and not only took down Gann, but gave us the key to finally finding Lara's answers."

"How?"

Attas grumbled beside him, and Medin shook his head. "You've waited long enough for answers to your own past. The future can wait a little longer. What else would you want to know first?"

Esta paused. "You said Old Garrow remembered us arriving in the slums. How come no one realized it was us until now? And what happened when... when our parents died?"

Medin lowered his head, and Attas cleared his throat before he spoke. "Your family was returning with other members of the court from Sahar, near the Shearpoint Mountains. Davin wanted Lara to see the Twilight Caves, one of the great wonders of our world. The border was relatively peaceful at the time. There had been no skirmishes with the Empire for many months. So for them to attack so deep into our lands, almost to Caroca itself... Their mage-fire consumed it all. There were so many we could never even identify..." He glanced at Medin, who was still staring at the floor. "All of us failed them. And we failed you, Rivan and Esta. None of us realized my brother's children had survived where all others had not."

"Stars," Rivan murmured. They all looked at him. "I, I thought they were stars. I remember. My mother put one in my hand, and it glowed in the dark. We were underground."

Attas smiled. "The quartz gems of the Twilight Caves are very special. They leave an impression on most who visit."

"You never told me," Esta said softly.

Rivan shook his head. "I didn't know. I didn't remember anything before the attack. Before..." She placed a hand on his trembling shoulder.

"Please," said Attas, his deep voice quivering as he rose and stepped towards them. "Forgive me. Had any of us known you had escaped, you would have been brought to me and kept safe. Raised as my own. We—I did not know. I am so sorry."

Esta dipped her head. She wanted to be angry. She wanted to scream at them both. Maybe kick over one of their fancy chairs pulled up to their fancy tables. She'd been subjected to years of fighting just to survive. Countless nights in bitter cold. Endless days in blistering heat, digging through the putrid refuse of the lowest slums. Fighting just to keep some shred of her own dignity under the nasty stares of drunkards and haughty eyes of nobles. It wasn't fair!

She looked up at her uncles, their eyes red. Tears welled in her own.

She couldn't. She just couldn't.

There was no bitterness in her as she saw them. Two broken men, her parents' grieving brothers. The only family besides Rivan she had left in the world. A family that wanted her.

Esta's breath came as a gasp. She ran to Attas, feeling his firm arms wrap around her as she sobbed into his chest. Her tears wet the king's robe, and his own fell into her hair.

"Esta, my dear Esta," he whispered. "You're home."

Chapter 7
The Ashguard

"Are you going to tell us now?"

"Are we there yet?" Medin marched down the corridor, perhaps a little more briskly.

"No."

"There's your answer."

Esta rolled her eyes. "Come *on*. You said they already know, anyway."

Her uncle turned down another faintly lit passage in the royal palace, leading her and Rivan farther into its depths. "I'm sure everyone could use a refresher."

She groaned, and sulked after them. It had been over a week since they'd moved into the palace, and Medin still hadn't revealed his plans fully to them. As delightful as it was having a huge bed to herself and all the warm baths she could want, Esta was growing restless. She also knew this pampered life was only a temporary reprieve. Something still had to be done with this mysterious job Medin kept hinting at. Only he seemed to be actively trying to avoid it, especially around King Attas.

"Hey!" she yelled as Medin's amber tunic vanished around another turn. "Wait for me!"

Esta caught him and Rivan just as her uncle pulled the handle of a wide door at the end of the hall. She hadn't been to this part of the palace yet, and the stillness of it was the first time she'd felt that familiar sense of unease since arriving. Most of Attas' grand palace was bright and filled with life. Dozens, maybe hundreds, of attendants worked diligently to keep the hub of Orda's government running. But unlike the rest, this wing of the palace sat ignored, almost intentionally.

Esta slipped into the gloomy room, squinting at the intense column of daylight pouring from the ceiling in the center. From what she could tell, its tan stone walls and floor were utterly bare, and none of the sconces were lit. The only feature besides the strange hole in the ceiling was the round, stone table its light fell upon. A large shadow beside the table moved, and she tensed.

"Took your time, Medin," came a deep voice, almost like a grunt to Esta's ears.

Her uncle strolled towards the table. "Well, someone decided to sleep in this morning."

"It's not my fault the bed is so comfy," said Esta, crossing her arms.

Her eyes widened as the figure moved into the light. He was the biggest man Esta had ever seen, dwarfing her uncle as Medin grasped the man's arm. His broad shoulders were nearly twice as wide as Rivan, bulging with muscle under leather pauldrons and a black, sleeveless shirt that looked like it would rip under the strain at any moment. His tanned face was pitted with scars, running over his shaved head. Esta's heart beat faster just at the sight of him. She edged closer to Rivan, who appeared equally intimidated. The man turned his beady eyes on the siblings.

"That them?"

"It is," said Medin.

"Hmph. Puny."

Esta's brows narrowed. The last drunkard to grab at her and call her that had ended up with a black eye and covered in his own drink.

She marched closer. "Want to say that again?"

"Es!" Rivan hissed.

The hulking man lumbered towards her, his ragged face twisted into an ugly grin. Esta craned her neck to scowl up at him, balling her fists at her sides. It didn't matter how afraid she might be. She knew better than to back down. If you rolled over in the slums, you were as good as dead.

"Brunce," said Medin sharply.

The man leered at Esta a moment longer, then relaxed. "Heh. Maybe not so puny after all. This might be more fun than I thought." Brunce trudged back to Medin, Esta still shooting daggers at his massive back.

Suddenly, the door behind them opened, making her jump. A pale woman with bright blonde hair pulled into a tight bun and ashen clothes glided into the room. Her ice-blue gaze swept over the others, landing on Medin.

"Artis," he said, folding an arm over his chest with a slight bow. "Did you find him?"

Her eyes narrowed. "Where he always is."

Medin sighed. "Naturally. Is he coming?"

"I am not his keeper," she said icily.

"Then we'll just have to begin without him."

Artis strode toward him, raising an arm with fingers pointed somewhere behind Esta. Light flashed from the woman's hand, and Esta flinched, blinded. Flame shot across the room with a hiss. Then another dart of fire. And another. By the time Esta had blinked the spots from her vision, all the sconces of the circular room were flickering, chasing away the gloom.

She's a mage! Esta stared at her, trying her best not to appear stunned.

Medin inclined his head. "Thank you. Now, Rivan and Esta, if you'll join us, I believe—"

The door slammed against the wall. King Attas stood in the opening, his nostrils flared and normally jovial face glowering.

"Medin, we discussed this," he said with an edge in his voice.

Esta's other uncle fixed the king with a hardened stare. "We did."

Attas stomped towards him. "I expressly forbade it! It is entirely reckless!"

"You granted me unhindered authority to lead this organization and its people as I deem fit," said Medin, crossing his arms.

"That did *not* include my niece and nephew! The willingness of you all to undertake your burdens is something I am forever grateful for." Attas nodded to Brunce and Artis before bringing his glare to Medin. "But I will *not* have my family cast into harm's way simply to sate your vengeance!"

Medin dropped his arms, his fists clenched. "This is not some petty quest for revenge, Attas. You know as well as I do that Orda's future may well hinge on this. Lara did not die just so we could lose this chance!"

Attas pointed a trembling finger at him. "And Davin wasn't killed simply for us to lose his children chasing some farfetched theory!"

"Stop!" Esta jumped between her fuming uncles. "What in Aldaria are you fighting about?"

Medin muttered under his breath and slouched against the table as Attas huffed.

"Is this about the job in the Empire?" she asked. "What does it have to do with our parents?"

Attas wheeled to Medin. "You already *told them*?"

"Not everything," he grumbled.

The king growled, rubbing his temple as he turned to face her. "Your uncle is convinced he now knows how to find the secrets your mother tried to give him. Even if he is correct, this plan places you all in terrible danger. It is a risk I am not willing to take." A fierce pain flashed across his weathered face. "I will not lose you and Rivan again."

"And if my sources and theory are right, how long do you think they'll be safe?" Medin slammed his hand against the stone and stood. "How long until the Empire marches on Caroca with unbridled power?"

Attas glowered at him. "You don't know that they will."

Medin flung out his hand, an object glinting in the light. "This tells me they will!"

Gann's ring.

"They *will* unlock its secrets. And the world will fall."

Esta gazed at its silvery-blue shard, shuddering at thoughts of that night. "I don't understand. What does Gann have to do with my mother?"

"Not Gann. The ring." Esta swerved to face Artis. The woman frowned, her piercing eyes locked on Medin's hand. "Its crystal holds magical properties unseen in all else of our world. Power unlike anything we have ever known."

Medin lowered his arm, his voice trembling. "Lara tried to warn me. Warn me that the Empire had found something. Crystals that could change everything. I didn't believe her."

Attas shook his head. "We don't know what the Empire is even doing," he said quietly. "We don't know whether these shards are a danger."

"Are you willing to stake the future of the free world on that?" Medin scoffed. "If the archon and his mages weaponize this, there is no power, magical or otherwise, that will stop them."

The king sighed, pulling at his peppery beard. "But... to risk so much on this one chance. To risk Esta and Rivan, Medin..."

"There is no mission, no hope of succeeding, without them," he said gravely. "Attas, I *need* them."

Esta stared at the ring in Medin's hand. Had her parents really died for something so... small? Trinkets she could fit in her hand?

No. Medin was right. Deep down, Esta knew he—and her mother—were right. Whatever this was, whatever the Empire was up to... It was big. Big enough to kill for. Big enough to orphan a little girl and her brother and ruin their lives forever.

Esta pushed down the cry forming in her throat. Every awful thing that had happened to her, including her parents' deaths, was their fault. Hating the Empire wasn't just on principle any longer. It was personal.

Her mother had tried to help. Had tried to do something. Now, what would she do?

Esta stepped beside Medin.

"I'll do it."

Her uncle looked at her, pain and pride written in his eyes.

"Me, too." Rivan slid beside her, wrapping an arm around her shoulders. Tears threatened to fall as she met his solemn look. "We're in this together. No matter what."

Attas fixed his gaze on Esta and Rivan. "So like them…" He let out a deep breath. "Very well. This decision is between you and Elowë above. I see it is not mine to make. If you are certain, I will not stand in your way."

Esta nodded. "We want to help. We want to finish what our parents started."

The king smiled at them sadly. "Davin and Lara would beam with pride for you." He glanced at Medin. "Your mission is approved, Lord Medin. I pray Elowë above sees each of you, my family, through it."

Medin bowed before Attas, then turned to Esta and Rivan.

"Welcome to the Ashguard."

Chapter 8
Plans

"Do you know the legend of the phoenix?" Medin asked.

Esta smirked. "I don't think you're allowed to be an Ordan until you've heard 'Dawn's Feathered Flame' bellowed from a barstool enough times that you can recite it in your sleep."

Medin raised a brow at her from across the stone table. "National anthems aside," he said dryly, "do you recall how they were said to be born?"

"Sure. They burned away when they died, and a new phoenix rose from its ashes. Honestly, it's part of why I still don't believe they were ever real. It's too bizarre."

Her uncle tapped his fingers on the stone. "You're lucky Attas left, or we'd be spending the next hour debating history and every farmer's wild sighting claim from the past ten years. But how do you suppose the creature became a symbol of our people?"

"Because they look impressive?" said Rivan, leaning into the light over the table. Medin frowned at him and looked back at her.

She shrugged. Flaming birds hadn't ever done her any good, unless you counted roast chickens swiped from street vendors.

Medin sighed. "I see there is room for improvement in your history lessons."

Suddenly, the door swung open, and a man staggered in.

"Good gracious! Apologies, my fair friends. I was, er, waylaid en route to our rendezvous. Have I missed anything?"

Artis sniffed. "Only everything important."

Esta wasn't sure whether to gawk or laugh. The man's black hair reached to his shoulders, matching his short, pointed beard. His ruffled shirt and fitted pants, complete with a narrow sword strapped to his side, reminded her of the tourney duelists that traveled through Caroca twice a year.

He strode over to Esta, taking her hand with a bow and a kiss before she even knew what was happening. "Lady Esta, no doubt. Honored. You are truly the image of your mother. Ah! And most certainly, dear Rivan. The spitting likeness of your father, if I may say."

Rivan gave the man a blank stare. "And you are...?"

Artis huffed. "Late. Again."

"Apologies. I am Arano Deshad," he said with a twirl of his wrist. "The greatest swordsman you shall ever meet. At your service."

Esta stifled a laugh. She wasn't sure if he really was the greatest swordsman, but he was entertaining.

"Well then," said Medin, clearing his throat. "If introductions are finished, I believe we were about to enlighten my niece and nephew as to the importance of Orda's historic symbol."

"Excellent, then I have arrived precisely on time," said Arano. "Carry on."

Medin shook his head. "As I was saying. Of all the wondrous attributes phoenixes were said to possess, it is their cycle that came to inspire the first generations of free Ordans.

"War has been the nature of our existence almost since the Hamid Empire and its Glorious Rule began. And there certainly has been nothing glorious about it thereafter. In the centuries that followed the Empire's formation, few nations withstood its conquest."

"Right. Only Orda and Neboa," said Rivan, folding his arms. "We know that much."

"Technically, the Anderfalls as well, if you count them as a nation," said Medin. "And there have been plenty of failed rebellions in the provinces. Though, only Fargost has been able to fully shake free of their grip. But I'm getting off course.

"Centuries of war brought its own cycle to Orda. If you peruse the recorded histories in the great library, you will see that Orda's experience with the Empire is defined by a pattern: war, destruction, rebirth. Time and again, terrible bloodshed between the two erupts, war devastates the nation, and from the ruins, Orda's people rebuild, their loathing and defiance of Hamidia only more solidified."

Esta's face brightened. "Reborn from the ashes."

Medin nodded. "But each cycle is costly, in many ways. When Fellinor rebelled one hundred and twenty years ago, its success—fleeting as it was—owed in no small part to Orda's war at the time, which held the archon's focus. Many Ordans died in those battles, but worse still were the traitors in our midst who slew the king and nearly claimed his sons. Had they succeeded, Orda may have fallen that day. So it was that after a season of reflection, a new institution was formed to ensure dangers lurking in the shadows would never again threaten the nation. The Ashguard."

"Which you are?" Rivan asked, gesturing to his uncle and the others.

"In part. The Ashguard has hundreds of eyes across Orda and the Empire, divided into smaller groups. Each team works together, always watching, always listening for whispered threats. We fight in the shadows so that one day, the war in the light might be won."

Esta tilted her head, her gaze sweeping Brunce, Arano, Artis, and her uncle. Artis, she could almost imagine as a secretive agent of the king. Her charming uncle, the flamboyant sword-swinger, and the lumbering troll-man, less so. "How did an Imperial from Araphon come to lead the Ashguard then? Because you're family?"

A somber expression came over Medin's face. "You are closer to the truth than you realize. By tradition, the Lord of the Ashguard, as so titled, fell to the king's oldest sibling. Where bonds between countrymen, and even friends, can be broken, it was believed their family blood would ensure the Ashguard never wavered in their diligence. It was the prince's greatest duty to keep watch over his king. To ensure that each cycle, Orda would rise again from the ashes as Aldaria's great beacon of freedom. And it remained this way, even through your father."

Esta bit her lip and pushed down the familiar, growing ache. "He was supposed to protect Uncle Attas then."

"And he did," said Medin.

"Until we failed to protect *him*," said Artis. A pained look crossed the woman's face. "We were Davin's group. We guarded one another. The day comfort replaced our focus, he paid the price."

"It is a burden we most certainly will all carry for the rest of our days," said Arano, somber.

"And why we now protect you." Brunce dipped his enormous head towards her.

"Protect us?" Esta looked at her uncle, confused.

Medin sighed, returning to the same grave expression he had given Attas before he left.

"I told your uncle the truth. I need both of you for this mission. But I don't like it any more than he does. I believe it is our one chance to thwart what the Empire is planning, but all of us will be in great danger. And none more so than you, Esta."

Rivan scooted closer to her, leaning farther over the table towards Medin with a hard stare. "What's so dangerous for my sister?"

Esta crossed her arms. "I think it's time you told us everything."

"You're right," said Medin. "But I need you to understand your history to see why this is worth the risk. Everything that has happened to you, to your parents... All of it comes to this. Elowë guided you here for a reason."

"There's no god in the sky moving my feet," she scoffed. "I can do that all on my own."

"Do you really think so?"

Her uncle stared at her, an echo of that pitiful look from beside the lake in his eyes. It made her insides squirm in a way she wasn't used to, and she'd seen and heard a *lot* of things that made people squirm. She pursed her lips and didn't respond.

Medin took a breath. "It took the Ashguard years to locate the man who sheltered Lara all those years ago. The one I knew was responsible for her death. And then it took longer still for us to learn his ways, to search out his weaknesses, and to lay the plans that would finally unmask him. He is shrewder than any of the archon's closest advisors, and far more ruthless. And his greatest strength is that no one would ever suspect him."

Esta wracked her brain, searching for any names she recalled of those leading the Hamid Empire. The archon had dozens of counselors, all of them powerful mages and brutal in their own right. Medin shook his head, as if he guessed at her thoughts.

"Lord Vintam of Ilagron. A man without magic."

Rivan snorted. "You're joking. If all this is as important as you make it sound, the archon would never trust it to someone that lowly. I've heard those marrying his highest advisors have to prove four generations of magic-wielders to even be considered."

"It's actually five. Which is what makes Vintam the perfect cover. You have made my point exactly, nephew."

Rivan scowled and pulled back from the table.

"Vintam was younger than Lara and me and has many siblings. He was not at the Academy when we were," Medin continued. "That made it difficult to track down exactly who he was. But once I was sure it was him, the question became how to infiltrate his estate. Whatever Lara found there, I'm certain still remains."

"You have a team." Rivan gestured to the others while still sulking. "Why us? Looks to me like you could've broken in years ago and been done with it."

Medin made a sound. "Vintam is no fool. He may not wield magic, but what he lacks in power he has made up for in intelligence and viciousness. He likely has to, among so many mages. His estate grounds are heavily guarded. Very little goes on inside it without his knowledge, and he rarely leaves. Another reason to believe the Empire's secrets remain with him."

"So, how do we get in?" Esta asked. Her uncle turned to her, graver than she'd ever seen him.

"*We* don't. You do."

Silence.

"Es—You don't," Rivan sputtered. "You can't send Esta in there alone! Are you insane?"

Medin ignored him. "Lord Vintam maintains a regular correspondence with Prince Avaj, a minor noble of Araphon. The prince's fortunes are dwindling, and he seeks to revive his trade influence in southern Hamidia, in which Vintam is the largest player. To date, there is only one price Vintam is willing to bargain for in exchange for access: the hand of Avaj's daughter, Isla. The princess's beauty is well known, though her father's protectiveness keeps her secluded, which has only increased the Araphon nobility's fascination. No doubt a few members of the archon's own court have heard her name. The Ashguard has ensured Avaj's correspondence offered her hand, and Vintam's own generous reply in turn."

"I'm the bait." Esta shivered. It didn't matter where they were. Nobles still played their games. Lives like hers and Isla's were just the pawns. Vulnerable pawns, and just as disposable.

Rivan slammed a fist on the table. "Absolutely not! You are *not* sending my sister into the hands of some sadistic Imperial!"

"Rivan," Esta murmured.

"This is the best you've got? Sacrificing her for some shot in the dark that this lord is behind it all? Attas is right. You're—"

"Rivan!" Esta grabbed his shoulder, forcing him to face her. "We agreed to this. If Medin is right, we could stop the Empire from doing anything worse. And even if he's not, it's one less life Vintam gets to ruin. I don't care if she is an Imperial princess."

"But, Es," said Rivan, "this isn't some Ordan noble we're tricking. This is the *Hamid Empire*. The same man who killed our parents!" He wheeled to Medin. "Vintam already killed our mother and father, and you're sending my sister straight to him!"

"Don't you think I know that?" roared Medin, fire in his eyes.

Esta flinched. She'd never heard him that upset. Her uncle slumped against the table, rubbing his temple with his face to the floor.

Rivan stood there, trembling, before he choked, "But why? Why her?"

"Only she looks the part of the princess, and…" Without looking at them, Medin pulled Gann's crystal ring from his pocket, laying it gently on the stone where it shone in the light. "Because she's done it before."

They all stared at it. A bright gleam in a room of darkness.

She'd meant what she said. Vintam had already ruined one life. Well, more than one. But now she had the chance to spare one. Maybe even ruin his.

"I'll do it."

"Es, no. You can't—"

"Rivan. I'm doing it." Esta clenched her fists at her sides. "Uncle Medin is right. I can do this. I want to do this. This man has walked free with our parents' blood on his hands for long enough. His time is up."

Rivan gaped at her, agony written all over him. She was doing it again. Taking risks and wounding his heart. She knew this job was the right thing to do. But that only made seeing his pain worse.

He hung his head and sighed. "Okay. You're right. I just... I don't believe it."

"What do you mean?"

Rivan met her worried face. "You called him 'Uncle' Medin."

She could've slapped him.

"*Rivan!*"

CHAPTER 9
TRAINING

A BEAD OF SWEAT trickled down Esta's neck. "Um…"

"Well?"

She stared at the utensils in front of her. *How in Aldaria did they ever keep all this straight*? It was akin to torture. She could've pawned the first seventeen for a decent catch and gotten along just fine with one. She shook her head. *No, I can do this.*

She grabbed the middle fork on the left.

Artis sighed.

Esta twisted around in her chair, her cheeks flushed. "I'm trying, alright!"

The mage rubbed her temple. "How have you survived this long without even an inkling of formal manners? That course was not served. It is the innermost that you need."

"Oh, I'm sorry. Should I have asked the rats if they preferred parsley on their crust? Or the pigeons to stop messing beside the table and fetch a napkin?"

Artis pursed her lips. "Again." She waved an arm, and all the silverware slid magically back into place. Ready to torment Esta with more failure.

She'd been training for weeks now with Medin's team. She knew infiltrating Lord Vintam's estate would require every skill and charm she had. What she hadn't anticipated was the whirlwind tour of every etiquette and stuck-up mannerism ever invented by nobles. Artis had been her instructor for those sessions, and even if Esta found the lessons tedious, the woman's Imperial expertise—and value to Orda—was clear.

Like Medin, Artis had her own reasons for leaving the Hamid Empire, and she'd remained tight-lipped about it, regardless of Esta's prying. The mystery, coupled with Arano's revelation Artis had been a prodigy even among the Empire's mages, only made Esta more fascinated by the strict woman. Still, she wasn't sure which she'd rather face: Artis' merciless power in sparring or her severe etiquette lessons.

Twenty minutes later, Esta stomped out of the palace's dining hall, still unsure whether it was the big fork or the one above her plate she'd needed. *Wait. Or was it the tiny one?*

"Hey! How'd it go?"

Esta snorted as Rivan stepped from the wide stairs to the upper floors and into the hall beside her.

"That good, huh?"

"Should I punch you now, or wait until we're outside?"

Rivan raised his hands, chuckling. "Alright, alright. Better save your energy for Medin, anyway."

Esta scowled. "He canceled. Again. Told me to meet Brunce."

"Huh."

"It's not fair! Why do you always get to practice swordplay with Arano, and instead of me learning anything *at all*, all I get is more hand slaps for grabbing the wrong spoon or a lecture on which mage-lord invented the flavor of tea the archon's court is raving about this week?"

Her brother shrugged. "I'm sure Medin has a reason."

As much as she liked her uncle, he was testing her patience. Medin was adamant that he manage Esta's training, but he continually canceled their sparring sessions. Of the few they'd had, Medin had only sparred with her twice, and then just for a few minutes before he called it.

Part of her was jealous that Rivan was receiving Arano's full attention. Surely, he could spare time and teach her something? He was, after all, the greatest swordsman she would ever meet, as he liked to remind her.

Esta continued glaring at the world as they exited the palace and entered the small training yard below, nestled between the palace cliffs and the king's gardens. Brunce and Arano were already there, chatting beside a pile of crates.

"Ah, Master Rivan!" said Arano, spotting them. He did his customary twirl and bow before snatching another sword resting on the crates. "We shall continue our duel from evening last. You nearly had a strike in your favor, so let us see how the Creator smiles upon you today. Perhaps there's a chance still. But remember, I am the greatest swordsman you shall ever meet. It is not a high chance."

Rivan smirked at Esta, then plodded after Arano to the far end of the field. She rolled her eyes and marched over to Brunce, the giant man still hunched atop the crates and studying her.

"Ready, small one?" he said in his guttural voice.

Esta crossed her arms. "For what? A history of Pelnoth bards? The Hamidians' latest silk slipper trend from Lynrest?"

"To test your strength."

The sneer dropped from her face. "What, against you?"

"Heh. Scared?" Brunce rose from his seat, towering over her in the arid heat. Sweat glistened on his shaved head.

Her heart beat a little faster. "I'm not scared! What weapons?" She glanced at the rack of poles, swords, and axes under a small, wooden pavilion at the edge of the yard.

"No weapons. Only bare fists and feet."

"Fine." Esta glared up at him. If Brunce wanted a fight, he'd get one. She kicked off her leather boots as he tossed his pauldrons onto the crates. She glanced at his enormous feet and bit her lip to keep from snickering. His toes looked like wiggling potatoes.

They stepped to the wide, grassy center, Esta doing her best to ignore Rivan and Arano in the distance, their dulled blades clanging. Brunce loomed across from her, rolling his monstrous shoulders with a grin on his scarred face. Esta bent her knees, waiting for him to move. She was wrestling a mountain. An actual mountain. She gulped.

I am so dead.

Brunce lunged.

She lurched to the side as his weight smashed into the earth. *Sweet Elowë, he'll flatten me like a leaf!* She threw her fist as hard as she could at his exposed side.

"Ow!" Esta yelped, shaking her hand. It was like punching a brick wall.

Brunce rose, leering at her. "Try harder, puny one."

His massive fist shoved into her stomach, knocking her back several paces. Esta ducked as he swung again, sliding underneath his arm and striking at his ribs. Again, her hands met immovable muscle. She kicked his leg, barely budging his stocky limb. His other fist came hurtling towards her, and she moved to block it. The force sent her teetering, pain vibrating across her arms.

Esta growled, springing at him. His hand caught her fist, trapping it in his own. She punched again with her other side, and he caught hold. No matter how she pulled, she couldn't break his grip. She bared her teeth.

"Let. Go!"

Esta felt herself being lifted from the ground by her arms until she was eye level with him. She kicked wildly at his chest, but Brunce only grinned.

"The bee doesn't fight the bear unless it wants to get squashed."

Esta gasped as he flung her away, and she tumbled into the grass. She sat up, panting. Her arms ached, and pain radiated from her side. She'd been in plenty of brawls in the slums. Never with a mountainous troll-man. There was always some weakness to exploit, though. He had to have something.

Brunce crossed his arms. "Give up?"

She staggered to her feet, seething. "You wish."

He chuckled. "Good. I was afraid you'd make this quick."

Quick. That was it.

Esta spread her legs, resting on the balls of her feet. Brunce crouched, then charged. He barreled across the lawn, the earth trembling. She dodged, whisking past the snap of his fingers. He turned to swat, and she ducked, weaving underneath his arms. Brunce swerved around, throwing another fist. Esta leapt past, deflecting his arm. He lunged for her again with outstretched hands. With nowhere to run, Esta sprang forward. She slid under his powerful legs, kicking against his backside as she rose. Brunce stumbled with a grunt.

He spun around with an astonished scowl. "You're quick. Smart. Like trying to catch a little bird."

Esta smirked. "Give up?"

Brunce laughed and prepared to charge.

"Well done," said a voice. Esta jumped as Medin stepped from the shadows of the pavilion, nodding approvingly. "Take a break, both of you."

"Next time, little bird," said Brunce with a gleam in his eye. He stomped back towards the crates.

Esta shuffled into the pavilion's shade, grateful for a respite from the sun's relentless heat. She hadn't won, but she hadn't lost either. *How many had managed that much?* she wondered to herself.

"You move fast," said Medin beside her. "That will help you. Always remember, sometimes the solution lies beyond your own strength. Don't be afraid to think creatively."

Esta nodded. Impersonating a nobleman's daughter and leading on one of the archon's closest advisors would certainly require some creativity. She shivered just thinking about it.

"I'd feel a lot better with a sword and some training," she said, eyeing him.

Medin shook his head. "Smuggling a weapon into the estate is an impossible risk. There is little good it will do you."

"Little good?" Esta echoed, rounding on him. "I'm sure I can find a weapon inside to use. But that's not going to help me if I don't also learn to use it."

"Esta, if you are resourceful enough to do that, then you are proving my point. Fighting will not make your part easier. It's your resourcefulness that will. The streets have taught you many skills; now you simply need to know how to act the part. Artis' lessons—"

"Those lessons aren't helping!" She put her hands on her hips. "What does it matter if I know how Imperials organize a boar hunt or who leads in a formal dance? I want to swing a sword. I want to know how to fight back!"

"No." Her uncle narrowed his eyes. "I had hoped a match against Brunce would sate your passion, but I'm afraid I've miscalculated. Your lessons are done for today. You may return to the palace and spend the day as you will until evening meal. You will meet Artis tomorrow morning in the library."

Esta stared at him in shock. "Seriously? You came down here just to dismiss me? What about our training?"

"That's enough for today, Esta."

Medin turned and walked towards the palace.

"Don't walk away from me!" Esta leapt in front of him, her hazel eyes blazing. "Don't you dare. You said you would train me, and instead, you're avoiding me! I haven't learned anything about using a sword. I know more about which dishes the Imperial court prefers for dinner than I do sword fighting! None of that is going to help me kill Vintam."

Medin's gaze hardened. "I have told you before. Killing Vintam is not our aim. Nor is it you fighting. If all goes according to plan, Elowë willing, you won't even raise a fist."

Esta inhaled sharply. "How can you still say that? He killed my parents. Your sister! Don't you want revenge?"

"Revenge won't keep Orda safe," said Medin, scowling. "Uncovering his secrets and revealing them to the world will. That is the end of the discussion, Esta."

Medin moved to pass her, and she blocked him. "*No.* I am not doing this job until you do what you said you would. Fight me!"

"Esta—"

"Now."

Medin glared at her, then sighed. "Very well. If that's what you want."

He strode over to the pavilion, wrenching two wooden sparring staves from the rack. He marched onto the field, tossing one at her. Still fuming, Esta snatched it from the grass and stomped to face him.

"Medin..." said Brunce.

"Enough." Medin's eyes narrowed at Esta. "Prepare."

Her knuckles whitened around the slender, grainy staff. It wasn't a sword, but she had asked for a fight. She'd used plenty of similar sticks in scraps before. It might even make her feel better to give her uncle a new bruise to consider.

Esta leapt, swiping for his neck. Medin moved as a blur, her staff whistling through the air where he had been. Suddenly, his staff slammed into Esta's legs, launching them into the air. Her back hit the ground before she'd even made a sound, knocking the breath from her lungs. She blinked the tears and stars from her vision as Medin's shadowy figure appeared over her.

"We're done." He stretched out a hand.

Esta could feel her face reddening. She slapped his hand away, crawling to her feet. "We're just getting started."

She raised the staff.

"Esta. We're done."

She swung.

Wood clattered. Medin glared at her, his nostrils flaring, and shoved her away. Esta sprang back as his staff sailed past. Again, he struck, Esta narrowly catching the blow aimed at her side with her staff before returning the strike. Medin parried, pushing her back.

Esta raised her weapon high, bringing it down with all of her might. Medin brought his up to meet it. Then, his arm jerked, and he froze, his staff falling to the grass as momentum propelled her own.

A sickening crack rang across the yard.

Esta screamed.

Her uncle lay on the ground, blood oozing from his head. She dropped beside Medin, afraid even to touch him. The others sprinted towards her. Brunce fell beside her, ripping off a piece of his shirt and pressing it into Medin's wound.

"Get a healer!" he bellowed. Arano dashed into the palace.

Esta stared at Medin, numb.

What have I done?

"Es," said Rivan, reaching for her.

She stood, every part of her cold and shaking, and ran.

"Esta!"

She sprinted away from the palace, away from her uncle bleeding into the earth. Tears stung her eyes as she ran, heedless of the pricks of gravel under her feet. *Why? Why did I force him to fight?* She ran until Rivan's shouts faded into the distance.

***

It was just as cool as she remembered. A world of blue serenity ringed in rustling emerald. The only peaceful place she could think of. It might as well have been a thousand leagues from all the damage she'd left behind.

Esta stared blankly at the lake past her dangling feet, watching the setting sun sparkle on the water.

She killed him. She knew she did. The man who offered her everything, the uncle she knew cared for her. She killed him.

Why? His staff... Esta looked at the puffy clouds drifting above. "Elowë, what have I done? I'm sorry. Please... Don't let him die."

Esta pulled her damp legs to her chest, a cry rising in her throat. She didn't deserve to be here. She wasn't family to the king. Even the slums were too good for her. After all, it dealt with murderers in its own way. She should just go back to them. Forget Medin had ever found her and let the slums decide her fate.

"Esta."

She gasped.

Esta turned, tears streaking her cheeks, still trembling on the stone dock.

Her uncle stood behind her with a length of cloth wrapped around his head, white contrasting against his black hair. He smiled at her gently.

"You're alive," she rasped, shaking her head. "You're... I–I'm so sorry. I didn't listen. I shouldn't even be here..."

Medin sat down beside her. She turned to face the lake and closed her eyes.

"You should hate me," she whispered.

He said nothing at first. He simply rolled up his pants and slipped his feet into the water.

"Why?"

"Medin, I *hurt* you. Bad. I was stupid and angry, and I took it out on you."

She tried to bury her face in her knees, but Medin's gentle hand raised her chin. He looked at her in a way no one but Rivan ever had. Not that pitiful face from the first time she met him here. It was something else, something more tender.

"Even among family, we still cause hurt. It doesn't mean we give up on each other," he said. "Es, you are my niece, and I will always love you. No matter what."

Esta sobbed.

Love.

Rivan showed it in his actions. No one had ever said it to her. Maybe she wasn't worthy of it, didn't deserve it. After all, she was a street rat. A rat who hurt people. Who could love that?

Medin's warm arms wrapped around her shoulders, and she cried harder.

He did.

Her brother did. Even the king did.

"I don't deserve love," Esta wheezed. "I deserve to be alone."

"Es," he murmured, "we choose to give love, not earn it. And you are never alone."

She rubbed her cheek. "I know. Rivan's always been there. He's my brother."

"Not just Rivan. Elowë is always with you. He always cares. You know that, right?"

Esta sniffed. "No. My brother's the only one who's ever been there for me, until now. I haven't seen a god in my life."

Medin squeezed her shoulder. "You might just find Elowë's been there all along, if you ask for eyes to see him."

She shook her head, scattering more tears. "How? After all the pain I've caused? After all I've been through and the Empire has done? How is *he* here?"

Her uncle pulled away, undoing the ties inside his amber tunic. "I mentioned how after they murdered Lara, the Empire came for me." Medin tugged down the top of his shirt and collar, revealing his shoulders. Esta took a sharp breath.

Massive, knotted scars ran across almost every shred of her uncle's back from his neck down. They bulged from his flesh, looking angry even while healed. She shuddered. How had he ever survived such maiming?

"This is why." Esta gulped. "This is why you wouldn't fight."

"I should have told you sooner. When a spasm takes over, I cannot control my own body. There are seasons, like these past weeks, when the pain is more active. Today is my fault as well."

Esta lowered her head. "I'm sorry."

"These are the stripes I paid for my silence," said Medin softly. "When the archon's Silencers came to my doorstep, dragging me from my wife in the night. Torturing me. Rending my flesh with magic. Demanding any scrap of knowledge Lara had shared with me. I refused to submit."

"Medin..." she whispered as he covered himself again.

He made a sound. "You asked how Elowë could be here. Analyn showed me how."

"Your wife?"

He nodded. "My father and his household are wholly devoted to the archon, and many past generations were adherents of the Imperial Cult. Analyn was different. Loyal, certainly, but she followed the Old Faith, followed Elowë. She embodied his teachings in every way.

"And when the Empire imprisoned me, Analyn..." Medin choked. "She came for me. Begged them to let me go. They had sentenced me to death, and she..." He covered his mouth. "She ransomed my life for hers. It didn't matter what I said in the end. They were convinced I knew nothing. And so, they let her, like some twisted game, then made me watch before tossing me into the streets."

Esta stared at him, speechless.

"They wanted to break me. To make me as vile as they were. I wouldn't. Not for Analyn. She showed me that day what true love is."

Her uncle sighed. "She personified it for years, and I took it for granted. But in that moment, I saw through her Elowë's own love for me and for his world. He gave of himself to fashion us and show us love in its truest form as an example. Like Analyn did. And so, nearly ten years ago I fled to Orda, searching for Lara's answers. To make Analyn's sacrifice worth more, and to trust that in all of it, Elowë was working some greater plan in which he had placed me here for a reason."

Esta shook her head, trembling. "I, I don't know if I could be like you. If I can believe Elowë has some purpose in it all. After everything the Empire has done to me, how could I not chase vengeance? How could I choose to love and not to fight?"

Medin's face softened. "Your parents chose to fight in their own way, as I did. To push back darkness, not out of vengeance, but out of a love for something beyond ourselves. The kind of love Elowë shows you and me. We fought for you and your brother. For the innocents of Orda. To give hope to a people wrapped in centuries of fear. He placed us here for that purpose. The question is not whether to fight, Es. The question is: what do you love enough to die for?"

Esta looked out at the water, rubbing tears off her skin. She'd fought her entire life simply to survive. Did whatever it took to keep food in her stomach and a roof over her head. What was worth dying for in the slums? *Only Rivan*, she thought. She would have for him.

But she wasn't in those dark, decaying streets anymore. She had a new family and new friends who, even though their lessons had been hard, still seemed to care about her. Even the troll-man, in his own way. Was she willing to die for them?

"Come on." Medin stood, stamping the water off his feet. "We should get home before Rivan raises a search party." He stretched out his hand. Esta smiled.

Home. She had a *home*.

This time, she took hold of his hand, letting her uncle wrap his arm across her shoulders and guide her through the shadows of the rustling trees.

Chapter 10
A Fond Farewell

Esta paced the far side of the meeting room, biting her lip as she toyed with the edge of her sleeve. The others murmured around the circular, stone table in the center, hovering over the maps and sketches scattered on its surface. She'd looked at most of them over dozens of times in the past month, so much so that she probably knew the grounds of Lord Vintam's estate by memory now.

What she didn't know, and what frightened her the most, was what waited within. She still struggled to believe Elowë was always with her, like Medin promised, but a deep part of her longed for it to be true. Once she went through those doors, she would be alone. And there would be no escape.

The door at the other end clicked open, and everyone hushed. King Attas entered, his jovial face resigned to grim determination as he strode to Medin in the center.

"Medin," he said with a nod.

Medin gave a curt bow. "It is all prepared."

Attas took a breath. "Then let us begin."

As Medin made room beside him at the table, he motioned for Esta to join the group. She edged closer, trying to hide her jittery nerves in the gloom between the light shining on the stone table and that of the flickering wall sconces.

Rivan gave her a concerned look as she settled next to him. "Es?"

"I'm fine."

"You're a terrible liar."

"Rivan, I'm fine." Esta scrunched her brows, focusing on the papers Medin was organizing as he muttered to Attas and Artis.

Brunce leaned onto the table beside her, more to put his face closer to her level than to relax. The table was still awkwardly low for him.

"'Course you are, little bird," he said, nudging her slightly. "You're ready."

Esta looked at him gratefully.

Medin cleared his throat, and they quieted. "Thank you all. I know everyone is well aware of the mission and its plan, but it is worth reviewing a final time. Today is the last time all of us will be together before its end."

Esta could feel the sidelong glances at her, and a knot formed in her stomach. It all began with—and depended on—her.

Thanks, uncle. No pressure.

Medin placed a finger on the large sketch of the estate grounds. "Vintam's estate, Giltcrest, lies in the hills southwest of the Hamidian city of Ilagron. There are a number of lesser properties around it, mostly other vineyards and orchards, and it is rather remote for an Imperial lord with the archon's ear. Lord Vintam also employs a sizeable force to patrol its grounds, which makes it difficult to enter unwelcomed."

"Good thing we're invited, then," said Brunce.

"For a time," her uncle replied.

"Did the others find any mages?" Artis asked. She crossed her arms over her ashen robe.

Medin shook his head. "Not that the Ashguard could confirm. Vintam's lack of magic makes for an interesting dynamic with other mages in the archon's court, but we should expect there could be some lurking in his staff."

"Esta." He turned to her, his normally relaxed appearance now gravely serious. "Your part in all of this comes first, and is the most pivotal. It begins the moment you step out of the carriage at the manor doors. Vintam believes Princess Isla, the daughter of Prince Avaj of Qumrar, is arriving early to prepare for their marriage celebration. To better acquaint herself with the lord and his estate. You must keep up this charade at all costs. While charming your way into Vintam's graces, you must discover where the Hamid Empire is hiding their research on the arcane crystals, and signal the team when it's time to launch our heist."

Esta nodded. "I, I understand."

"A thick forest borders the western end of the estate grounds," continued Medin. "Rivan will watch from there at sundown each night for your signal light that it's time to move in. The team will work out the best route to infiltrate the grounds while you work on discovering its secrets."

Rivan placed his hand over hers. "We're in it together, Es. I'll come the moment you need us."

Medin swept the group with a serious look, lingering on Esta. "Time is the most fragile piece of this plan. Esta, you will have two weeks to find Vintam's research and signal the team. The real Isla and her father will arrive for the celebration then, and we must be well on our way back to Orda before your deception is revealed."

She stared at the maps, thinking. "Have the other Ashguard found any more ideas on where to start looking? I doubt Lord Vintam has a big sign for 'secret evil workshop. Keep out.'"

Her uncle smirked. "Unfortunately, no. Lara was not specific in what she told me, and they have found nothing further than what we've already discussed. But I believe this has some role to play in it."

Medin pulled Gann's crystalline ring from his side, placing it on the table. "You'll notice the shard has been cut in rather odd places, giving it a series of tips at the cardinal ends. It may be part of something else in the Empire's research, as other influential figures connected to Vintam are believed to be in possession of similar trinkets. Take it with you."

Esta tentatively reached across the surface, taking the cold ring in her hand. Just seeing it brought back memories of that horrid night. *Please don't let this job be as bad as that*, she silently prayed. She didn't know if Elowë heard her, and it was hard to hope. After all, they were taking on the Empire.

"Just remember, keep it hidden. Keep it safe. Vintam must never know you bear it."

"And once the dastardly Empire's secrets are in our grasp?" asked Arano, leaning against the table.

"Flee. As quickly as you can," said Medin. "Vintam will be consumed in preparations, and he will not risk revealing more about what he's been doing to Prince Avaj or the other dignitaries by chasing after you himself."

"I thought Vintam was an outsider in the archon's court," said Esta. "Just how many dignitaries are we expecting?"

Artis sniffed from across the table. "Did you think our lessons were for nothing?"

"Only sort of," she muttered.

"The wedding of an Imperial lord, even a minor one, draws attention," said Artis. "Many other members of the archon's court will be in attendance. You will need all the knowledge and skills we practiced. Be aware, other lords with larger entourages will also be arriving early."

Esta sighed. *Great. Now there are more of them.*

"Play the part as you must, but focus on Vintam," added Medin. "He'll want to look good in front of the others. You must get the secrets out of him, and he's more likely to slip under their added pressure."

Esta nodded.

"Your plan is no less risky than before," grumbled Attas, "but it is sound. This is the best chance we've had to infiltrate the Empire and learn the truth behind these crystals. And armed with their knowledge, perhaps for once we will be ahead of their scheming and able to strike back. What you do here will ensure generations of Ordans remain free of the archon's tyranny, and your bravery cannot be honored higher. I only wish it did not place so many of you in such danger." His deep eyes studied Esta, and then Medin.

"We all do," said Medin quietly.

"Esta, if you would." King Attas gestured for her to join him. She slipped around the others, her boots echoing awkwardly in the silence. Though, maybe only to her. It felt as if every eye was on her again. Her heart beat nervously as the king placed his hands on her shoulders, beaming.

"My dear niece. So much has changed in the past few months since you came to us, and I am so proud of all you have and will accomplish. I did not ask you to take this burden, but you have done so willingly, on behalf of me and all of Orda. You are, in so many ways, the embodiment of your parents' greatest qualities. Thank you, Esta."

Attas bowed his head to pray, and Esta mimicked it. She snuck a glance at her brother, surprised to see even Rivan had lowered his head.

"Father of All," Attas began, "we thank you for the life you give and the passion you've inspired in these men and women. They represent the greatest of your attributes: valor, sacrifice, and love. Protect them as they embrace the purpose you've given them and contend with darkness that light may be shown. Guard their steps, and bring them safely through trial. Grant each of us peace, knowing that at your side awaits an eternal glory for those who trust in you, no matter how dark the world seems to become. We ask this in your name, Elowë." The king sighed deeply. "So let it be."

The group whispered among themselves as King Attas embraced her a final time. "Never forget, you are loved by me and all of our family," he said. "I truly am so proud of you. Even when you fear, trust Elowë. Be the light, like Davin and Lara. I know you will."

Esta nodded, trembling, as he squeezed her shoulders. "I, I love you, too." Attas smiled gently, and stepped away.

Had she really said that? Was a broken, little girl from the slums of Caroca really capable of love? Maybe. She didn't have another word to describe the way she felt, rubbing the corner of her eye as Rivan and the others circled over to her.

"We've got your back, Es," said Rivan, giving her a side hug.

Brunce grinned, wrinkling his scarred face. "You're fierce, little bird. Vintam won't know what hit him. Maybe you'll punch him yourself. Save us the trouble."

She laughed. "Maybe so."

"Faugh! A brawl?" scoffed Arano. "Nay, give them each a sword and have it out properly. Esta, milady, there is a single move which I can show you to unhand the scoundrel with ease. One only the greatest—"

"Yes, yes, Arano," said Artis, frowning. "But our chance depends on stealth, and on Esta's natural charm. *They* are her greatest weapons when wielded properly, especially when alone."

"Not fully alone."

Esta turned as Medin approached the group. The others drifted towards the table as her uncle studied her.

"The carriage will be here soon to take you to Ilagron," he said. "Everything you need has already been prepared."

She nodded absently, another knot forming in her stomach.

"You'll do fine," he said with a kind look. "We all believe in you."

"Thank you. It's just..."

"You're afraid."

Esta bit her lip. "Yeah."

Rivan was right. This wasn't some Ordan noble. One wrong move, one wrong word, and she wouldn't live to see past Vintam's walls again.

"You would be foolish not to be. But sometimes, Elowë uses our greatest weaknesses and fears to create something more magnificent than we could imagine. I believe he will do it through you, Esta."

"Thank you," she said quietly, lowering her gaze.

"And as I said, you won't go alone. I'm coming to Ilagron."

Esta's head snapped up. "You... you're coming? But—"

Medin raised his hand. "Just to drop you off at the estate. They'll expect a servant to assist with the luggage. I won't be able to stay, but I could never send you off entirely on your own."

Esta threw her arms around him. She knew the job still depended on her, but part of her simply dreaded the journey there, trapped in the solitude of her own anxiety and thoughts as doom neared. Now, her heart leapt, knowing she wouldn't face it alone.

"But... can you do that?" she asked. "What about your, um, condition?"

Medin shrugged. "The pain has eased this past week. I should be fine for a while as long as everything stays... cordial. I'll join the team once you're in, to help finalize the plan to get everyone else inside."

Esta felt as if her grin couldn't get any wider.

"Oh, there's just one more thing." He smirked. "But you aren't going to like it."

Her smile vanished.

"It better not be another stupid dress."

Chapter 11
Gilded Shadows

Esta sat, bracing herself against the door of the gloomy carriage as it rattled down the dusty road. It was stuffy and hot. More like a shaking cage than a luxurious ride. Why in Aldaria did nobles insist on them? She growled as another bump ruffled the fold of her stupid cream and claret dress. She'd take Ordan fashion over Imperial any day. The bodice around her slender chest felt like a torture device. *Do Imperial noblewomen* really *wear these all the time?* At least Medin hadn't made her wear it since practicing with Artis until they'd passed through Ilagron. She stretched to smooth down the dress's rumpled edge.

"Ow!" Esta rubbed her head where it'd knocked against the carriage frame.

"Sorry!" Medin called from above. He leaned over from the driver's seat to peer through the window. "Doing okay in there?"

"You might have to find Vintam a new bride if we don't get there soon. I'm about to be rattled to death."

Her uncle laughed. "Looks like the Empire doesn't have much interest in maintaining roads south of Ilagron. But we're almost there. Should be over the next rise."

For a moment, Esta forgot about the annoying carriage. A twinge of fear filled her, and she pressed against the door to look out at the green hills and vineyards rustling in the midday breeze. It had taken them weeks to skirt the clashes at the Ordan border and circle around to Ilagron, the largest city in southern Hamidia. Medin had quizzed her endlessly on Lord Vintam, the estate, and Imperial nobility, which had passed the time, but only just. Now they would see just how far the practice would carry her.

Esta's eyes widened as the carriage rolled over the hill, and the estate came into view. Rows of grapevines stretched in either direction from the center lane, reaching to the gentle hills at the property's northern and southern ends. A sea of purple lavender swayed along the path beyond the fields, bordering the manor lawn. The great manor itself towered over the pristine grounds. Its pale, chiseled bricks, tall windows, and gilded embellishments gleamed in the sunlight. Stone paths snaked towards smaller outbuildings on the grounds, everything from the servants' quarters to stables fashioned with the same immaculate stonework, though more subdued than the estate itself. Past the grand building, a long pond glistened before the emerald of a dense forest, stretching to the western horizon.

"Beware the beauty," said Medin as Esta blinked away her awe. "Even evil can wear a golden mask."

Anxiety churned inside her as they passed through the glittering gates and into the estate. Vintam's manor was breathtaking, to be sure, but it didn't take her uncle's warning or the years of staring at Caroca's upper district for Esta to feel the dark undercurrent she was drifting into. Soldiers in polished armor along the lane marked their movement. Servants in the fields didn't dare look up. Under the brightness of the day and her surroundings, instinct told her Giltcrest's loveliness was as hollow as a rotting tree.

"Whoa." Medin pulled the carriage to a stop before the lofty double doors of the manor. Golden wolf heads leered at her from their carved timbers, shining as the doors opened and figures scurried from the shadows inside. Male attendants in buttoned coats and maids in cotton dresses lined the doorway.

Esta took a breath. *Alright, Elowë. Medin says you put me here for a reason. If that's true, tell me you'll get me out alive.* Her uncle scrambled down from above and opened the door. *Please.*

Esta stepped carefully into the sunlight, grateful to feel the fresh breeze again. She nodded to Medin as he straightened his tawny servant's vest and moved to fetch the luggage.

"Welcome, Princess Isla!"

Esta jumped, turning her attention to the manor. A man in a silk waistcoat and pants with gold embroidery strode towards her. His blond hair was pulled behind his fair, angular face. He was older than her, as she'd expected, though she was surprised at how his confidence complemented his appearance rather than projecting arrogance. He walked with a determined step, stopping before her with a slight bow. His dark, gleaming eyes met hers.

Esta curtsied, as Artis had shown her. "Lord Vintam."

He smiled. "The days until your arrival could not pass soon enough, my lady. Welcome to Giltcrest Estate. We are honored to have you join us."

She nodded politely. "As I am honored, and I could not agree more. The land here is beautiful, as is your manor."

"Indeed, though not as beautiful as yourself." Esta blushed as he continued, "We strive for perfection at Giltcrest, something your father will no doubt appreciate when he joins us."

"Oh, yes," said Esta. "He most certainly will. My father sends his regards and regrets he could not come sooner for the preparations."

Vintam waved his hand dismissively. "By all means. I, for one, understand the demands leadership places upon him. There are many burdens on Prince Avaj's shoulders, and our union should be a cause for celebration, not add to them. But rest assured, everything is precisely on schedule for the festivities."

She beamed at him. "Wonderful. I have been looking forward to this day for so long now."

"As have I." Vintam returned her smile, an intensity burning in his gaze. Something about it unsettled her. "But! No doubt you have endured a lengthy and uncomfortable journey. You must be exhausted. Please." He motioned to a pale woman in the lineup, and she hurried over with a bow. "Show Princess Isla to her chambers and have her belongings brought up."

He looked at Esta once more, taking her hand with a bow. "I am delighted to have you here, Princess. I will see you for dinner once you have had a chance to acclimate."

She curtsied and turned to follow the maid into the manor as the other attendants moved to assist Medin by the carriage.

"Why, do I know you?"

Esta froze. She spun back, terror gripping her chest as Vintam cocked his head at Medin while her uncle fumbled with one of the bags.

Medin straightened and bowed. "Apologies, my lord. I do not believe so."

"Hmm. Your face seems familiar, but for the life of me, I cannot place why."

Esta made a tittering laugh, drawing Vintam's attention. "Oh, him? He's served my father since I was a child. Many have said that. It must be something about his looks."

"Perhaps." Lord Vintam frowned, as if trying to recall a detail he'd forgotten. "Apologies, princess. Do not allow me to keep you." He glanced at Medin. "As you were."

Vintam strode past Esta into the estate, disappearing down one of its airy corridors. Esta stifled her relief and hurried after the maid, not daring to draw more attention to her uncle.

Her heart still beat wildly as Esta passed into the towering foyer. Polished marble floors swept from the entry through doorways into more halls, and up two curved stairways to the upper floor on either side of the central corridor. Gold sparkled from everything: the grand chandeliers, the railings, the trim along the pale, paneled walls, and even busts of grim-looking men in alcoves underneath the stairs. As luxurious as King Attas' palace was, it paled in comparison to Giltcrest. The extravagance of it all nearly made her dizzy. *Just how wealthy is Vintam?* Esta wondered. She shook away her awe and followed the maid to the second floor.

More halls of polished floors and gilded walls ran in each direction. Beautiful paintings of scenery and proud figures, as well as rich tapestries, hung over the spaces between the manor's many painted doors. They passed dozens of rooms, concealing even more of the estate's luxury and untold secrets.

"How large is Giltcrest?" Esta asked with a hint of wonder.

"There are forty-eight rooms in the manor, excluding common areas such as the reception rooms, dining rooms, library, and also excluding the lord's private quarters," the maid answered as she led on.

"So many, and so quiet. I will get lost in its halls."

The woman paused in front of a painted door. "Many guests will arrive soon for your wedding celebration, princess. It will not feel so quiet then." She opened it and motioned for Esta to enter. "And all of the manor staff will be delighted to assist you whenever needed."

Esta stepped into the chamber. A thick, muted rug spread across the sitting room floor, its white pattern matching the walls and fabrics of the room's furniture. Golden trim and fixtures gleamed on every side, reflecting the warm light streaming through the windows to her right. Through a columned archway, she could see the design echoed in the large, gilded frame of the bed and the mantle of a fireplace. She could hardly believe this room was hers. It was meant for royalty. Or perhaps it was meant to inspire awe, if one didn't first find it intimidating.

"The evening meal will be served one hour before sunset, princess," said the maid, drawing Esta's gaze. "The chambermaid will be here to assist beforehand, and I will return to escort you to the dining room. If you need anything before then, please use the cord here by the door to ring for assistance."

"Of course, thank you."

The woman curtsied and left the room. A moment later, Medin staggered in, followed by a pair of manservants, all carrying luggage. They set the bags down inside, and the two men bowed before disappearing, leaving her and her uncle alone. He put his hands on his sides.

"Leave it to an Imperial lord to put you at the very back of the manor," Medin said, panting.

Esta grinned. "Not cut out for servants' work?"

"Out of practice." Medin lugged the bag into the bedroom and returned. "Remind me to thank Artis for insisting we keep up all appearances, including hauling a full wardrobe for you."

Esta smirked at him before thoughts of Vintam sobered her.

"That was a close call," she said, lowering her voice.

Medin frowned, a hint of worry in his eyes. "I knew better. I'm endangering the mission. I shouldn't have come."

Esta stepped closer to him. "Why? Has he seen you before?"

"No. Lara."

"Oh. I didn't think..."

Her uncle shrugged. "It was two decades ago, so who can say? But I think it's best that I don't linger."

She nodded, biting her lip.

Medin placed a gentle hand on her shoulder. "Will you be okay?"

"I'll be fine." She hadn't survived years of thieving in the slums to back out on a job like this. Especially now, knowing Vintam's role in her parents' fate. "Tell Rivan not to worry."

He chuckled. "I'd have better luck telling a rooster not to crow. But we'll be ready. Just be careful."

"I will."

Medin smiled at her and bowed. "Elowë be with you, Princess Isla." Then, he quietly left the room.

Alone.

Esta shivered, holding the backs of her arms as she stood in the warm light from the windows and looked out at the gardens and hills beyond. She'd run plenty of jobs solo with Rivan in support. Her innocence and charm made her the perfect insider. But for the first time, she felt truly alone. Willingly trapped inside a gilded cage. Even on the Gann job, she knew Rivan was just outside the walls of the estate. Here, against a powerful

Imperial lord and his band of soldiers, could they really pull it off? Could *she* pull it off?

Please, if you're there... Esta glanced at the bright sky. *Be with me.*

Chapter 12
The Boy

"It is incredible," said Esta, mustering an astonished look. "And you run all this by yourself?"

Lord Vintam chuckled, fixing the ruffled end of his sleeve as he shut the door to the winery. "Goodness, no. There are many foremen who oversee each step of the process, and many more managing the other operations of the estate. All of whom report to me." He extended his arm, and Esta obliged, secretly loathing the way he led her across the manicured grounds towards the manor.

"But my wine is the most sought after in all of Hamidia, including for this year's Festival of Triumph. It is a high honor," he continued. "And all of it requires an army both to oversee and to produce what is needed to meet the demand."

"And still so young." She tucked a strand of her dark hair behind her ear, gazing at him. "How have you accomplished so much from a simple vineyard?"

Vintam smiled at her. "Winemaking is but one of my many ventures."

"Will I get to see these many ventures on our little tour?"

He patted her hand. "All in good time. There is much to show, for there is much I pursue at our archon's pleasure. And he rewards perseverance generously."

She looked at him with surprise. "Then, Archon Tibris is a patron of yours?"

"Come now," he said with a meaningful glance. "Your father knows that well enough. The archon has interests well beyond the capital city of Agonar. And mine is a poorly kept secret by all regards."

Esta shrugged. She hadn't often wondered about the vast capital of the Empire. Even while knowing it still lay many days' journey north of Ilagron, the thought of already being closer to the schemes of the Empire's ruthless ruler at Giltcrest unnerved her. "Alright. It is just startling to hear it confirmed. The archon always seems so..."

"Distant? Ensconced on high behind his mage-lords?" He smirked. "You might be surprised. And before you ask, I know what is whispered out of my presence. None of it matters. Only Tibris' opinion does. And yours." He stopped outside the back doors to the manor, letting go of her arm to face her. The perfect hedges and flowering trees of the gardens rustled behind him as his dark eyes studied Esta. "Does it bother you?"

She shook her head. "Of course not."

"You may be honest. My life is to be yours, after all. I will not diminish the challenges of being one of my stature among a court of mages, or those of becoming my wife." He gazed at her with that same intensity as before. Esta's stomach churned, and her pulse quickened. She shoved it aside, placing a gentle hand on his arm.

"Magic, or lack thereof, does not define you. It's what you do with what you are given that matters."

Vintam raised his brows. "I did not expect a scholar besides beauty. As well said as any among Fountmore's brightest, Princess Isla. I am indeed a lucky man."

Esta beamed at him as Vintam took her arm once more and escorted her inside, resisting the urge to pull away.

What in Aldaria had she just said? Was she being *nice* to him? The man responsible for murdering her parents? He didn't deserve nice. He deserved a dagger in his back.

But Medin was right. If Vintam died, so did the secrets her mother gave her life for. She needed him close. For now.

"Ah, the hall of statues," he said, pausing as they entered the room.

Esta's eyes widened at the expansive hall, its bare marble floor and gilded walls gleaming under rows of crystalline chandeliers. A dozen bronze statues of men in lavish robes lined the interior wall across from the tall windows overlooking the gardens.

She looked at Vintam coyly. "Is sculpting another of your business avenues?"

He laughed, strolling towards the nearest one. "No, I cannot count myself so talented. These replicas of the archons, rather, are a memento of Giltcrest's former occupant. An odd obsession perhaps, but I couldn't bring myself to dispose of them. I have always found them fascinating."

Esta let go of him, studying the grim, wrinkled face glaring down at her. She even disliked dead archons. "Interesting. And... former occupant?"

Vintam pursed his lips, cocking his head to the side. "It does not do to displease the archon, but those who *prove* their loyalty reap the benefits." The way he said it made Esta's blood run cold.

His face brightened. "Still. This room will make a wonderful reception hall after our ceremony. Don't you think?"

Esta swallowed, channeling her fabricated eagerness. "Oh, absolutely! It's perfect."

His teeth flashed as he extended his hand to her. "Perhaps a bit of practice for our dance?"

She blushed, hesitantly raising her arm. "Oh, I'm not sure it's proper. This dress. Lord Vintam, I—"

Vintam grabbed her hand, pulling her to him. "My dear. Vintam will suffice."

Her heart pounded against his chest as he placed his other arm behind her. They waltzed across the sparkling marble, Esta scarcely able to breathe as she focused on keeping her feet from tripping.

"A natural," Vintam said. She squirmed under his gaze, nervousness creeping up her spine as he held her tighter, a glint of hunger in his eyes.

Run. Push him off and run. Instinct screamed at her, but Esta felt frozen, locked in his grasp.

"My lord!"

Esta jumped as Vintam stopped and glared at the door as the steward hurried through its open doors. "What is it?"

"My lord, Archmage Savos has arrived," said the steward, bowing. "His carriage is pulling up to the manor as we speak."

Vintam frowned and nodded. "I will be there at once." He turned back to Esta, releasing her from his embrace. "Forgive me, I must see to one of our guests. But I will spare you the dull affair until our celebration. Shall I send the maid to escort you to your rooms?"

"No, that is quite alright." Esta shook her head, partly to conceal her trembling. "I will manage."

Vintam looked at her, amused. "Of course. Giltcrest is your home now. We did not finish our tour of the gardens. You might find the labyrinth an enjoyable challenge."

Esta forced a smile and curtsied. "Thank you, my lord... Vintam."

With a grin, he kissed her hand, then disappeared down the hall. Esta released the air from her lungs, clutching her stomach to calm herself. She wanted to be somewhere, anywhere, but here. *Outside. Out of this cage.*

She hurried out of the manor and into the sunlight streaming across the paved terrace overlooking the gardens, letting the gentle breeze and rich scents of the flowering shrubs waft over her.

Actually, Vintam's suggestion didn't sound so bad. Right now, she wouldn't mind getting lost in a garden labyrinth. Esta stepped down onto the path between the foliage and headed for the high hedgerow, and the columns signaling its start.

The moment she slipped past the chiseled stone of the maze's entrance, Esta felt like she'd entered another world. The quiet buzz of the estate, and even the bird calls from its trees, vanished beyond the lofty hedges. She sighed, thankful for a respite in the shadows after hours of being led about by Lord Vintam. Esta wandered on, aimlessly losing herself in the twisting paths, but frustration slowly tempered her relief.

She'd spent an entire day with the man and still had no clues about the Empire and its research. Everything Vintam had shown her, from the manor gallery to the winery, was opulent but mundane. Nothing but Vintam's own veiled coldness seemed to prove Medin's belief in something more nefarious happening at the estate. *It's only been a day,* she told herself. *I have to give it time.* Except time was the one luxury Giltcrest wouldn't afford her.

"Leave me alone!"

Esta jumped as the small voice pierced her brooding thoughts. A mean child's laugh followed with the patter of feet on the gravel path. Suddenly, a small boy shot around the turn ahead, nearly barreling into her. He gasped, stumbling. Brown, shaggy hair hung around his face, the pale cheeks below his blue eyes smudged with tears. He quickly wiped them away with a hint of fear.

"M–milady," he stammered. Scornful laughter echoed off the hedges, and a moment later, two boys, slightly older than the first, raced around the corner. They froze the moment they spotted Esta.

"That's her," one of them muttered, nudging the other. "The lord's bride." Dread spread across their dirty faces.

"Sorry, princess," said the second, a skinny, blond-headed boy with a sunburned nose. "We didn't know anyone was out here." The boy who'd nearly run into her sniffled and stepped back.

Esta raised a brow, trying to look her sternest. "And what is going on here?"

"N–nothing, princess," said the blond-headed boy. "Just a game." The other stifled a snigger, poorly.

Esta narrowed her eyes at the pair of them. She knew that face the littlest boy wore. She'd worn it a hundred times back home. It didn't matter whether it was a bully in Caroca's slums or on the grounds of an Imperial estate, they always tormented someone smaller than them.

"Leave," she said coldly. "I don't want to see either of you making trouble again, or you'll regret it."

Terror seized them. "Y–yes, princess." They bowed and sprinted past her, not daring to even glance in her direction. The first boy made his own bow, then turned to chase after them.

"Wait a moment," said Esta. The little boy froze, worry painted on his face as he looked at her. She gestured to the maze ahead. "Why don't you walk with me?"

The boy glanced from side to side as if it were a trap. "Um. Okay. I mean, yes, milady."

He shuffled back to her, tugging at the corner of his dingy shirt. His small shoes were practically falling apart, and a layer of dirt stained his faded clothes. Esta guessed him to be around nine or ten years of age. But the way he walked, and the look in his eyes, reminded her of Rivan from their childhood. She wouldn't wish that on any child.

"So," she said as they strolled along the shadowy path, "what's your name?"

"Jack." The boy rubbed his face again, trying to wipe away the streaks.

"It's nice to meet you, Jack. I'm Isla."

He gave her a bashful glance. "You're, you're the princess. From Araphon."

Esta smiled. "That's me."

Awe filled his small face. "But that's so far away. I–I've never been farther than Ilagron, but the others say it takes a month to reach Araphon. Maybe more!"

"It can," she replied with a laugh. "I suppose it depends on how you're traveling. You've really never seen beyond Ilagron?"

Jack shrugged, relaxing slightly. "I've only been there a couple of times. Whenever Cook takes me to help."

Esta looked at him quizzically. "You work in the kitchens, then?"

"Sometimes. Cook likes my help, mostly. Sometimes, the grownups make me do other chores."

"Do your parents work at the manor?"

He dipped his head, turning somber. "Cook raised me. Says she needed a helper. I don't know who my mom and dad were."

"Oh." Pain tugged at Esta's heart. An orphan. Like her. "And... those other boys?"

Jack frowned, his cracked lips trembling. "They're always mean to me. Sometimes, I get extra food from the kitchen, and they know it. They'll take it if they can, but today I ate fast. They didn't like that."

She halted. "Why doesn't Cook stop them? Or the others? Surely someone..."

He shook his head harder. "No. No. Cook says it's not her problem. The other grownups don't like it when I bother them. They... They don't want to be my friend."

His lips quivered like he was on the verge of crying. Then he took a breath and raised his small chin. "It's okay though. I'm good at hiding. Usually."

Esta stared at Jack as he ambled on, forcing away the tears forming in her eyes.

He was her.

She could see them. She could still see the grimy, sneering faces of the boys shoving her into the muck, wrenching scraps of stale bread from her little fingers. Their mocking chants as they chased her with sticks through the alleys after stealing the coin she'd spent hours begging for. She could feel the cold rain trickling down her shoulders and knees hugged to her chest, whimpering under a broken awning as the pain pulsed on her cheek. Until Rivan showed up. Until her big brother repaid their bruises and sent them running.

Only Jack didn't have a Rivan. No one came to stop his torment. No one came to rescue him, to pick him up, to offer a hug. He was alone, truly alone. And this gilded estate was a cage he could never escape.

Jack was her. A shadow of her broken past replaying itself in another's world.

Esta clenched her fist. *No.* She refused to let that happen.

She strode after him, placing a hand on his sagging shoulder. Jack flinched, spinning around nervously. Esta lowered herself to his level, meeting his fearful stare with the softness of her own.

"Jack, would you like a friend?" she asked. His blue eyes brightened. "Would you be *my* friend?"

He nodded his little head vigorously. "Yes! I... But Princess Isla—"

She held up a finger, her eyes twinkling. "Ah, first rule of friendship: no 'princess.' Just Isla. At least, when no one's around."

Jack grinned. "Okay."

"Rule two: Stick close to me as long as Vintam isn't in sight. No bullies allowed on my watch."

He giggled. "I like that rule. But shouldn't you say 'Lord' Vintam?"

"Oh, I suppose. Anyway, the third rule: any secrets stay between us. Deal?"

"Deal," said Jack, shaking her hand very businesslike. "I know lots of secrets."

Esta gave him her own mischievous smirk. "I'll bet you do." She glanced up at the towering hedges. "Now, my friend, do you have one for getting us out of here?"

"Yeah, it's this way!"

His small hand tugged her on, weaving through the maze of greenery. He practically radiated joy, skipping across the gravel, heedless of the world around him. Warmth filled Esta's chest. It was such a small thing. A gesture to the lowest of lows.

"Princess Isla!" the steward's voice echoed beyond the labyrinth.

But she knew. To be called a friend was the longing of her own childhood heart, the one only Rivan had ever filled. To Jack, she knew it meant the world.

Jack froze as the columns of the entrance appeared at the end of the hedges.

"Princess Isla!"

He turned to her, worried. "Will I get in trouble if they see me?"

Esta shook her head. "Brave Sir Jack, rescuing a princess from the dark forest?" She squeezed his hand. "Not on my life."

Together, they strode into the light beyond the maze. The steward and head maid spotted them immediately, scurrying past the colorful flowers and rustling bushes towards them.

"Oh, thank goodness," breathed the steward, patting down the strands of graying hair across his balding head. "Lord Vintam has been most anxious about your whereabouts."

The steward frowned, noticing Jack for the first time. "And what are you..." His face hardened as Jack sheepishly slipped his hand from Esta's. "Step away, boy. I will deal—"

Esta turned to Jack, stooping to wrap him in her arms. "Oh, thank you so much! I was afraid I would never escape that maddening place." She pecked him on the cheek, and Jack blushed. Though his face wasn't nearly as red as the steward's. "My hero."

"Y–yes, well," stammered the steward. He cleared his throat. "Thank you, boy, for escorting the princess to safety. Now, we really must return to the manor."

"Indeed. Dear me, the time!" added the maid. "Princess Isla, we must get you prepared for the evening."

Esta stood, brushing off her dress. "Of course. Please, lead the way."

The servants turned and hurried towards the estate. Esta glanced back at Jack, standing awkwardly by the hedges, and winked. He grinned, giving her a small wave, before he darted through a row of bushes towards the servants' housing and disappeared.

CHAPTER 13
HUNTING RUMORS

ESTA PICKED UP THE paper fan from the small side table between their seats, waving it as fast as she could while maintaining her composure. Heat shimmered outside the curtains tied to the poles of their pavilion. Even in its shade, she felt smothered. Her tight-fitting dress certainly didn't help matters, but she'd taken pains today to look her best. Not just to keep Vintam's attention, but because it was her first real outing with the other nobles since she'd arrived at Giltcrest Estate earlier that week. And it hadn't taken long for Esta to realize the Empire's elite played their own games with words as dangerous as any duel.

"Madness," said Comtesse Mirabelle on the chaise beside hers, Mirabelle working her own fan in the still air. "Leave it to men to insist upon chasing hideous, hairy pigs through forests for the sake of some competition, and in this scorching heat. Hmph!" The woman pursed her lips, tugging at the crow's feet beside her gray eyes.

"Oh, come," said Lady Morven, a younger noblewoman Esta had only met that morning. "You know as well as I it is simply an excuse for them to tout their own boldness in front of each other."

"True, though I must agree with the comtesse. Today's excursion has been far less pleasant than the hunt Baron Navan hosted," added Lady Katrin, dabbing a handkerchief below her blonde hair pulled up in elegant braids.

Comtesse Mirabelle raised a brow, her eyes gleaming. "Ah, yes, I remember. And how is the young Sir Perivan? A pity he could not attend the festivities this time. I imagine his new bride is keeping him quite busy."

If Katrin's looks could kill, Esta expected the comtesse would have collapsed where she sat. She didn't need all the background to know the older woman had pricked a tender wound. But from what Esta deduced, Mirabelle held some influence within the archon's court, and so far, the others would only duel with her to a point.

Lady Katrin grumbled. "Well, at least he escaped this unseemly heat."

"Giltcrest is simply too far south," complained Lady Morven. "Much less tolerable than Agonar. And besides, it is so near to those beastly Ordans." Esta stiffened, quickening her fan.

"Indeed," said Mirabelle with a conceited look. "Most unpleasant. Though perhaps this place suits you, Princess Isla." The woman turned to Esta, who froze. "I hear anyone who dares venture into the heat of the Great Desert perishes before the hour has passed. I would think living at its border simply ghastly, had I not at least some climatic affinity."

Esta opened her mouth to speak, but Morven cut in. "Oh, my! How dreadful. Do they even have sport in Araphon? Perhaps hunts for those sand dragons in the bards' songs?"

Esta shook her head, shifting her legs under the stifling dress. "Oh, no. They are much too dangerous, and normally too deep within the desert to even attempt."

"Those tale spinners spout enough fantasies about romance without you believing their grandiose accounts of monsters," said Comtesse Mirabelle, fixing Morven with a disapproving frown. Morven looked as if she'd been whipped.

"But we do have other traditions," added Esta, pulling their attention off the pitiful girl. "And ways to ease the harshness of the desert. High Prince Ibhrar hosts the most luxurious affairs at his palace in Aljardin, and all of his guests leave more refreshed than when they arrived."

"Yes, it is a shame Fellinor is not closer to Giltcrest," said the comtesse, switching hands to continue her fanning. "I have heard the fruit ices the high prince serves using its imports are divine."

I take it all back, thought Esta silently. *Your lessons might save my life, Artis. Thank you.*

"Why, who needs Fellinor?" said Katrin. "That would hardly be a trick for any of the mage-lords. If I recall, Lord Erlin's ice sculpture in the challenge last winter—"

"Was a farce," said Mirabelle, scowling. "He did not even complete its backside. My husband's, however, was immaculate."

"Of course. Count Wilhelm's display was superb. My point simply was, my dears, why not make our own? We could call one of the men back from the hunt to make the ice, and Princess Isla, I am sure, can assist in fashioning one of these enchanting refreshments."

"Oh, well, I—"

"Actually," said Katrin, ignoring her, "come to think of it, where is Lady Evie? She is just as capable, and more reliable, than the men. Archmage Savos went out with the party this morning."

Morven shook her head. "His wife remained behind. The lady was feeling ill and has not left her chambers. I expect it was the trip."

"A pity Lord Vintam is not so gifted," said Mirabelle, eyeing Esta with a gleam. "No doubt with your beauty and at your word, he would forsake the hunt in an instant."

"Very unfortunate," added Katrin, giving Esta a sympathetic look. Though, Esta suspected it wasn't entirely genuine. "He has shown so much potential. It is a shame his deficiency thwarts his advancement in Agonar."

"Deficiency?" echoed Esta.

"The lord's lack of magic, my dear," said Katrin with a sniff. "A terrible curse. But you have handled yourself gracefully in such unfortunate circumstances, being matched to him. Thrust upon you, to be certain."

Annoyance simmered in Esta's stomach. She hated Vintam, but the arrogance with which other members of the archon's court seemed to walk left her loathing them just as much. Clearly, they would prod at her just as much as at one another. *Well, two can play at that game.*

"My lord's favor with the archon appears no less than the others," she replied. "The contract for this year's Festival of Triumph was awarded to Giltcrest, after all."

The other women stared at her in disbelief. Esta looked at them innocently. "Oh, I assumed... Forgive me. When Lord Vintam told me of the news, I assumed it had been announced to the court."

Lady Katrin sat up, her face reddening. "I, but my father was certain his position this year was secure. His holdings are closer to Malgavorn, after all. You, you can't be serious."

Comtesse Mirabelle tittered. "My dear Katrin, compose yourself. I am certain the princess meant you no disrespect." She glanced at Esta with a hint of newfound esteem. But just a hint.

"Well, Vintam *is* wealthy," said Morven modestly. "You cannot discount him for that."

Lady Katrin huffed. "Not if his shipping business continues as it is."

Esta perked up. Vintam hadn't mentioned that. "Shipping?"

"Yes," said Mirabelle slowly. "It seems his business has dwindled as of late. Several of his contracts have passed to Lord Aragoz and Lord Prospen. From the outside, Lord Vintam appears to be neglecting his ventures. He rarely leaves the estate these days."

"I see plenty of Giltcrest caravans passing through Agonar," said Lady Morven.

"Yes, yes, but most of them end up here," said the comtesse irritably. "Most curious. It is rather difficult to profit from yourself."

"Caravans for what?" Esta asked, almost too eagerly.

Morven shrugged. "How should I know? After all, it is not *my* husband's business."

Esta sat back against the cushion, staring at the forest rustling ahead of them. Vintam was moving something. Wine? Not to himself. The Empire's research? Maybe. And if it was arriving at Giltcrest, it had to go somewhere on its grounds.

Esta sighed. *If only I weren't getting married right now.* Wagons appeared almost daily at the estate, ferrying supplies for the upcoming celebration at a dizzying rate. It would be impossible to figure out if something was coming in for other purposes without staking out every shipment. And she doubted Vintam would simply leave her alone long enough to do so. She needed another way.

"Princess Isla."

The small voice startled her from her thoughts. She turned to find Jack standing beside her chaise with a silver pitcher clutched to his chest. In his new servant's outfit, he almost looked like an entirely different boy.

"Oh, yes. Thank you, Jack." She had almost forgotten he'd disappeared to the manor before their conversation set in.

Carefully, he poured cool water into the silver glass on her table, then moved to offer a drink to the others.

"Very well," grumbled Comtesse Mirabelle, nodding to her own glass.

After refilling each of the women's drinks, Jack stepped beside Esta and bowed, flashing her a small grin, before disappearing once more.

"Princess," said Mirabelle with another of her disapproving looks, "why do you insist upon having that urchin attend to you? Surely one of Lord Vintam's footmen is capable and more... presentable."

Esta gave a small shrug. "He is far quicker. I believe it is the youth."

The comtesse studied her with a frown before turning back to Lady Katrin in conversation.

It was partially true. Jack had a way of vanishing and reappearing the moment you needed him. Reality, though, was more complicated. The time she'd spent around Jack and learning more about him over the past several days had only made her more protective of the boy. And the other boys didn't dare approach him, knowing she was around.

But Jack also knew things about the estate. He knew which overseer was misappropriating funds from the winery. He knew which chambermaid the steward was pursuing, without success. Jack even knew Lord Vintam despised rats and had his room inspected for them every evening before retiring. Jack saw what others didn't, because no one saw *him*. Esta's face lit up.

That was it.

She didn't know which shipments might be for the Empire's research, but Jack would. And if he didn't, he could find out.

She bit her lip. But asking him to spy could be risky. Of anyone at the estate, Esta felt like she might actually be able to trust Jack the most. She'd even considered telling him her real name out of guilt for the lies she kept repeating. It wasn't the risk to her or the mission that worried her. It was the risk to him.

"Ah, Lord Vintam," said Comtesse Mirabelle, startling Esta from her thoughts.

The lord strode across the grass from the trees to their pavilion, handing his gloves to the steward following him, before wiping a handkerchief across his brow. He bowed before the group, flashing a charming smile before his gaze settled on Esta. She forced a smile in return.

"Fair ladies. Are you enjoying your respite?" he asked.

"Very much," answered Lady Katrin. "The manor grounds are lovely today."

"A bit warm," added Comtesse Mirabelle, still waving her fan, "but I must concur. The gardens are blooming nicely this year, Lord Vintam."

He inclined his head. "My apologies for the weather. We can only hope someday even the sun bows before the archon's will."

The comtesse laughed. "If Tibris' might could reach that far, I do believe the Imperial Cult may need restoration."

"New discoveries always lie on the horizon, my lady." He glanced at Esta. "You never know what surprise may be next." Esta continued smiling at him, a knot of worry secretly forming within her. Something told her his words weren't a passing remark.

"Well, how fares the hunt?" asked Mirabelle. "I suppose my husband is still out there, likely ruining the shirt I just had sent from Lynrest in some wild chase. You *did* pair him with Savos again."

Vintam chuckled. "We shall do our best to preserve it, though our luck has been scarce today. Actually, I was hoping to borrow Princess Isla for a moment, if you would indulge me."

Comtesse Mirabelle's eyes gleamed before she waved a hand. "Off with you two lovebirds, then. But only for a moment! You must chase down my husband next before the evening preparations."

He bowed. "Upon my honor, comtesse. Princess?"

Vintam stretched out a hand, and Esta took it, thankful for a moment away from the warmth of the plush chaise as she stood. He guided her leisurely from the others, towards the gardens under the baking heat. Esta wished she'd at least taken the fan with her.

"Well then," he said once they were out of earshot. "How go pleasantries with the court ladies?"

"Very well," replied Esta, meeting his serious gaze. "They have been... welcoming in the manner I am sure is expected for an occasion of this kind."

Vintam raised a knowing brow. "Then you have outlasted their trial by fire."

"I am a quick learner." Esta shot him a sly grin.

He chuckled. "As I expected. Still, should you encounter something disagreeable, do let me know. I will see that it is... corrected."

Esta shook her head, her nerves rising. "I will manage. Though, surely you didn't pull me away to examine the conversations of court women?"

"Perhaps simply to steal a moment with my beautiful bride?" He pulled her arm closer to him, and she felt the color rising in her cheeks. In any other circumstance, he would've been face down in the dirt with throbbing shins. As it was, she endured the closeness with a blush.

"I suppose I'll allow it," she said shyly. Vintam studied her, his intense gaze holding her eyes in its depths. He moved his arm behind her, pressing her into his side. Esta didn't need the instinct telling her he was dangerous. He wrote it in every move he made. His head inched closer, and her insides squirmed. Suddenly, he froze. The passion in his eyes faded into a grim look.

"Actually, I must ask your forgiveness," he said, leaning away. "I am afraid I will be absent from our evening activities."

Esta's heart still pounded. "Oh? What's happened?"

"Nothing of concern," he said. "There is a business matter I must see to in Ilagron before the day is over. I do regret leaving you at the mercy of the court at the evening meal, however."

She looked at him, trying to appear hopeful. "Perhaps I could accompany you and see more of your exciting ventures?"

Vintam shook his head with a smirk. "You would find this one rather dull, I'm afraid. Rest assured, I will return before the morning meal tomorrow." He patted her hand. "You will hardly know I am gone."

Esta dipped her head. Part of her truly was disappointed. Whatever he was doing could be another clue to the research. On the other hand, she now had an evening free of his continual presence. If only she could slip away from the other nobles. *I just need to find Jack.*

"Now," said Vintam, turning to face her as he moved to hold her hands, "I have kept you long enough. You have an evening with the comtesse to prepare for, and I have her stubborn husband to track down in those woods. I am certain he still has not located his lost boar."

Esta laughed lightly, then turned somber. "You promise you will not be gone long?" she asked.

He gently squeezed her hands. "I will come back to you as swiftly as I may."

With a final bow and kiss of her hand, Vintam turned and strode back towards the pavilion and the forest in the distance. Esta let out a sigh of relief, then stepped hurriedly towards the manor. Halfway through the manicured shrubs and flowers of the gardens, she froze at a rustle to her left before a boy's shaggy head popped from the bushes.

"Jack!"

He cocked his head at her. "The lord looks at you funny. Like he likes you, but more. I don't like it."

Esta glanced around them. The gardens were empty. "You noticed that, huh?"

"Do you like him?"

Even in the heat, she shivered. "I... It's complicated. Look, Jack, you promised to keep our secrets, right?"

He nodded his little head, his brown, tangled locks swirling. "Yes, always!"

"I need to ask you something, but not here. After the evening meal. Is there somewhere we can talk?"

Jack looked thoughtful for a moment. "Yeah. We can go to my hideout!"

Esta smiled. "Perfect. Where should I meet you?"

"Your rooms. I'll come get you."

"You're not supposed to be in the guest wing, though." She frowned at him. "What if you're caught?"

Jack shook his head, grinning. "There's a secret way. I'll be fine."

A distant laugh startled Esta, and she peeked over the shrubbery towards the pavilion where the other women were rising from their seats.

"I've got to go," she said. "Tonight. I'll slip away from the others as soon as I can."

"I've never shown anyone my hideout," said Jack, his eyes wide with excitement. "You'll love it!"

"I'm sure I will." She smirked at him and waved before his tiny figure darted back behind the shrubs, and his little steps faded deeper into the grounds.

Esta turned and continued walking towards the manor, trying to keep an even pace as her heart raced and stomach churned. She was a step closer to answers, and a step closer to danger. All she had to do, all she could do, was ask for his help. But her one question risked everything. She only hoped Medin and Rivan would understand.

Chapter 14
The Request

Esta paced across the rug, fiddling with Gann's crystal ring in her hand. She'd exchanged her stuffy, formal dress from the evening meal for a more breathable gown after excusing herself early under the pretense of weariness from the day's heat. She must've played the part well. Even Comtesse Mirabelle appeared sympathetic. She glanced at the moon shining through the windows of her room. *Where in Aldaria is he?*

She jumped at a creak in the silent hall and shoved the ring into her pocket. Everyone should have been downstairs, still conversing in the grand sitting rooms with their wine and stories from the day's hunt. Esta inched closer to the door, and a soft rap knocked against its painted frame. "Princess?"

Esta flung open the door as quietly as she could. "Jack!"

The little boy smiled and gestured to the hall. "Hi! Follow me."

She trailed after him, casting backward glances down the corridor. If anyone came around that corner, there'd surely be questions. After passing a couple of other rooms, Jack stopped next to a solid, paneled wall. He reached for the long edge of the paneling, and with a soft click, a section of it no larger than Esta's hand tilted away. She gaped as cracks formed in the wall and the hidden door swung open, revealing a dark, musty stairwell.

"Come on!" said Jack cheerily.

"What is this?"

"Oh, the old servants' passage. Steward Gambold says they used these before Lord Vintam took over. But then the lord wanted the staff only moving where he could see them."

Esta stared at him, wide-eyed. "You mean no one uses these passages at all?" She stepped into the gloom beside him.

Jack shrugged and pushed the door shut. "I don't think so. It's against the rules. But as long as no one sees me, I use them to hide." A dim light filtered down from the stairs above, strengthening as Esta's vision adjusted.

"Where else do they go?"

"All over," said Jack, hurrying up the stairs. "You can get from one end of the manor to the other and only leave the passages three times. That's when you have to be extra fast."

She shivered in the chilly darkness, groping forward after him while trying not to trip. *Vintam's secrets could be in here!* she thought to herself. *Why else would he forbid the staff from using them?*

"Here we go," said Jack.

Esta looked up to see his small body clambering up a ladder towards a hole in the ceiling. Stars twinkled above his silhouette, momentarily blocked as he swung through the hatch.

"Come on!" he whispered. "I made sure everything was ready before you came."

She stepped onto the ladder, shifting to pull her dress from under her shoe. "Stupid dress," she muttered, hoisting herself higher.

She grasped the edge of the opening, then pulled herself into the moonlit darkness of the night. A soft breeze ran across her bare skin, filled with the scent of the lavender fields. She hugged her arms close, blinking at the sight. They were on top of the manor, nestled behind the chiseled bricks and gilded embellishments walling in the building's edges. The estate's property spread in every direction, its fields rustling in the gentle wind.

"Well? What do you think?"

Esta turned. Jack beamed at her in the moonlight, kicking his legs against a battered crate covered with a patched blanket and sitting against the parapet. A small table of sorts sat beside it, the top fashioned from a sun-bleached board over an overturned box. An assortment of rocks, glass shards, feathers, and more covered it like a miniature display.

"This is my museum," said Jack proudly, gesturing at the collection. "I hide all my best stuff up here, because no one knows about it."

She smiled at him. "It's wonderful."

It really was. She closed her eyes, forgetting the chill for a moment as the wind washed over her in the silence. For a moment, it was as if she stood in Caroca, feeling the breeze above the slums, letting the night air fill her lungs as she swayed above the rooftops. In all of its hardships, the crumbling rooftops were the one place where she'd truly felt free, unshackled from the struggles and dangers of the streets.

She sighed. Giltcrest and the slums. Two sides of the same coin. Both cages, one rusted, one gilded. She'd simply traded one for the other by taking this job. But maybe Medin was right. Maybe somewhere in this new cage, she could finally do something that mattered. Something more than just her own survival. Something she needed the help of a small boy for.

Esta sat down beside Jack on the crate, rubbing the backs of her arms.

"Oh, sorry," he said sheepishly. "Here." He pulled a small, tattered blanket tucked between him and the parapet and extended it to her. She wrapped the weatherworn fabric around her, grateful for the warmth. It didn't matter that it smelled. It reminded her of home.

"Aren't you cold?" she asked.

Jack pulled up his legs and shrugged, trying to mask a quiver. "I'm okay."

Esta rolled her eyes. "You're a terrible liar." She moved closer to him and threw the blanket's edge around his shoulders.

He stared at her in awe. "I–I never thought I'd get to show a princess my hideout. And never that she'd like it."

She looked at him gently, feeling that familiar twinge of guilt that'd nagged her now for days. If she were truly his friend, Jack deserved to know. But knowing meant dragging him into her mission. It meant asking the question she both most feared and most needed to ask. It meant putting a child in harm's way.

What would Vintam do if Jack were caught somewhere he shouldn't be? Vintam had already killed her parents and Elowë knew how many others to keep his secrets safe. What was the life of one urchin to him? But Esta was running out of time, and she was utterly alone. She needed help. And Jack... Esta let out a breath.

Jack looked at her, concerned. "What is it?"

Her uncle's words came back to her, unbidden. Medin believed Elowë had put him where he did for a reason. If she was going to believe in Elowë or any of it herself, then the same had to be true for her. "And it must be true for you," she murmured, gazing down at the boy beside her.

"What? What's true?"

"Jack." She folded his small hand in hers. "Can you keep a big secret?"

His little eyes widened, and he nodded seriously. "Yes, I promise."

Esta swallowed. "I... I'm not a princess, Jack."

He stared at her, confused. "But the grownups said the lord was marrying a princess."

She gave a small nod. "He is. But it's not me."

"Then... who are you?" His little form edged away from her.

"Your friend, and someone who needs your help."

Esta looked at him pleadingly as Jack studied her for a moment, scrunching his face. Then he nodded. "You're my friend. My only friend. I won't tell anyone."

She squeezed his hand. "Thank you, Jack."

"But why do you need my help?"

Esta bit her lip. There was no going back now.

"Something dangerous is going on at the estate, something that could hurt a lot of people," she said. "My friends and I need to find out what Vintam is doing."

"But the lord does lots of things. What are you looking for?"

Her hand fell against the ring stowed in her pocket. Slowly, she pulled the glittering shard and gold into the light. Suddenly, Jack gasped and scooted away.

"That's one of the bad men's rings." He shook his head, pulling his legs to him. "Are they your friends?"

"No! No," she said, covering the ring. "I'm trying to stop them."

The boy relaxed, inching closer to her again. She looked at him with worry. "Jack, you've seen one of these before. Why are you afraid?"

His lip trembled. "I always hide when one of them comes. They always come alone, only to see the lord. One of the other boys got in the way one time. The man hurt him. And... and the boy died. The lord made the groundskeeper bury him, and yelled at his father."

Esta's blood ran cold. Was Vintam really that heartless? Was keeping his secrets and prestige with the archon really worth tolerating *that*?

"Jack," she said in a low voice, "I want to make sure that never happens again. But to do that, I have to stop whatever Vintam is planning. I need to find the secrets he's keeping at Giltcrest. Something related to the shards in these rings." She slowly revealed the ring again, letting its faint, silvery-blue light glow against her palm.

"I–I don't know where the lord and bad men go when they meet. I stay away," said Jack, still nervous. "Sometimes, they go to his study, like the others who visit. But then they always disappear."

Esta nodded. "I think they're moving more of these shards to Giltcrest, probably wherever Vintam disappears to. I need to find out where the shipments are going, but I can't watch everything coming into the estate without him becoming suspicious."

Realization spread across Jack's face. "But I can. Most everything comes to the servants' entrance at the side by the kitchens. I've watched lots of stuff for your, er, the princess's, wedding come through."

"Would you know if it was something different?"

He thought for a moment. "I think so. Most of the deliveries go to Cook or the steward for the storerooms. They don't notice me. I could follow them if they went somewhere else."

"Jack, I don't want to get you in trouble or put you in danger." Worry filled her as she looked at him. "You can tell me no, and I'd understand." She wouldn't even blame him. She'd never helped anyone on the streets except Rivan.

Jack shook his head. "No, I can help. You're my friend."

Relief washed over Esta, mingling with the guilt still brooding inside her. "Thank you."

"So..." he said, looking at her awkwardly, "if you're not a princess, is Isla your real name?"

She grinned. "I can't get anything past you now, can I? No, my name is Esta."

"It's nice to meet you, Esta," Jack said, smirking.

"Only let's keep it to 'Princess Isla' outside of your hideout, hmm?"

"I will. Oh! It's like we're secret agents of the Empire now. We have a mission to complete without the bad men finding out."

Esta wasn't sure whether to laugh or gape at him in horror. "Well, something like that."

And what would these 'bad men' and the Empire do once she'd been unmasked? Medin had a plan to get the team safely away to Orda, but Jack... *Oh, Elowë. What happens to him?*

"There's one more thing," she said, pulling his attention back from his daydreaming. "Vintam is going to be angry when I'm done. At a lot of people."

"I'm good at hiding," he said, like she'd forgotten. "I'll stay out of his way."

"No, I don't think that's a good idea. Jack, what if... what if you left Giltcrest?"

He looked at her in confusion. "Left? But this is the only place I know. Where would I go?"

"I..." She stopped. *Why didn't I think this through sooner?* she thought to herself. She couldn't leave Jack to endure Vintam's wrath, and she couldn't push him into the unknown. There was only one answer.

"You could come with me."

"To... to live with *you*?"

"Yeah." Esta slowly nodded.

The thought of Jack safely in Attas' palace with her and Rivan filled her with a mixture of happiness and excitement. He could be free of Vintam. Free of the estate and its bullies. Free like her uncles had made her. Maybe Medin was right. Maybe there really was more to her coming to Giltcrest.

"There'd be no more mean chores from grownups or bullies to hide from. No more being alone. You're my friend, and I would keep you safe, Jack. No matter what."

A flash of longing crossed Jack's face before worry clouded it. "I would like that. A lot. But... The estate is all I've ever known."

"I understand."

And she did. Jack leaving Giltcrest was like her leaving Caroca's slums. The king's palace had sounded like a dream, an impossibility. She'd been betrayed and told enough lies to make second-guessing instinct. Part of her had been just as scared to believe it could be true.

She squeezed Jack's hand again. "Just think about it for now, okay?"

He flashed his little smile at her. "Yeah, I will."

Esta glanced at the twinkling sky and moon above them. Concern rose inside her. More time had passed as they talked than she'd realized.

She sighed. "I should get back to my room before the others retire."

"Cook is probably wondering about me, too." Jack dropped from the crate, and Esta followed.

After carefully descending the ladder into the darkened servants' passage and shutting the hatch, they groped their way down the stairs, heading for the small glint of light peeking below the hidden door to the guest wing. Esta waited as Jack fiddled in the dark for the handle, then blinked as warm light flooded her vision. She peeked into the hall. Clear.

"Thank you, Jack," she said, stepping lightly onto the marbled floors. "And just... be careful."

He bobbed his head in the gloom, excitement and nervousness radiating from his small face. "I will. I'll find you as soon as I see something."

With that, Jack closed the hidden door, sealing Esta in the flickering light of the gilded hall. Esta turned, heading as casually as she could for her room.

She'd done it. She'd made her request and put things into motion that couldn't be undone. Esta knew she should be thankful. Instead, she felt terrified.

Elowë, she prayed, looking beyond the windowed hall at the darkness, *please tell me I'm doing the right thing. Please keep Jack safe.*

Then she turned the golden handle of her door and slipped inside.

Chapter 15
Secrets

"My dear princess, you simply must try this."

"Oh?" Esta jerked her head up as Comtesse Mirabelle motioned for the servant. A delicate glass of amber liquid was in her hand before she could even object. "I—thank you."

Esta took a polite sip, letting the drink burn its way down her throat. It didn't seem to matter how exotic the wine was. All she could taste with each drop was the bitter concoctions from The Hog Pen that Rivan had dared her to try. The fact that the comtesse continued to impose upon her many of Lord Vintam's special vintages only made the memories more poignant. She silently cursed the grimy tavern for ruining her.

"It is lovely," said Esta, tightening the corners of her lips.

"I know it is unlike the familiar wines of Araphon," continued the comtesse, "but that is all the more reason to accustom yourself. After all, you will be surrounded by them here at Giltcrest and at all the functions of Tibris' court. Think of this evening as your first real soiree."

Comtesse Mirabelle smiled as she gestured at the crowded room. In only a week since Esta's arrival, it seemed half the archon's court had arrived at the estate, fully prepared for what Lady Morven had termed the 'pre-festivities.' Esta preferred to call it what it was: self-aggrandizing nobles impinging on Vintam's winemaking ventures. Not that she cared if they drained his winery before the week was through, as long as she could be left out of it. *Not a chance in Aldaria*, she thought to herself.

"Ah, you found the four-fifty for her, then?"

Esta turned as Lady Evie approached from another huddle of brightly dressed noblewomen. Esta curtsied. Though Evie was not as old as Mirabelle, the comtesse appeared to hold the archmage's wife in high esteem. Something of a feat, it seemed. Probably because Archmage Savos was Archon Tibris' closest advisor. Though Esta wondered what that implied about the archon's relationship to Vintam, and Mirabelle's own veiled determination to keep Esta close when Vintam didn't have her. *More games and posturing.*

"It was a fine year for wine," replied Mirabelle, smiling. "I expect even the grapes celebrated the number of slain Ordans on the border that year."

"Paired with the recapture of Fellinor, who could blame them?" Lady Evie laughed, taking another glass from the serving man.

Esta grit her teeth and forced a smile of her own. Living on the streets hadn't exactly made her an ardent loyalist, but Orda was still her home. And now, knowing who she actually was, what King Attas and Medin were really like... She took another sip and let its burning sensation linger like the anger in her chest.

Lady Evie smoothed the edge of her sapphire dress, her chestnut eyes scanning the crowd of heads. "I say, where are the others? I at least expected Lady Morven to stick close. We would be far better company than enduring Lord Trevan's flattery of yet another baroness."

Mirabelle made a sound. "Quite true. Poor girl. It is admirable how she abides him. But I expect she will cement her name to the rights of Castle Neurim before the year is out. Then we shall see who truly holds the power in western Agonar."

Evie raised one of her slender, chestnut brows. "You truly think so?"

The comtesse scoffed. "Why else in Aldaria would she remain? She is already so close to achieving it. Lady Morven will gain a seat on the Imperial Council, and then Trevan will find himself quite disposable."

"Well. A woman without magic on the Council. That *is* a delicious morsel."

"Oh, speaking of which." Mirabelle patted Esta's arm. "We simply must find that man with the oysters. Another bit of fascinating cuisine from Pelnoth to accustom yourself with. Ah, of course, Count Hargev has cornered him. One moment." The older woman slipped off into the crowd.

"Has Lord Vintam let you out of his sight, then?" Lady Evie asked, casually observing the noisy hall.

"For the moment," said Esta. "I expect he will return momentarily."

She rather hoped he didn't. The only time Esta hadn't been in his presence for the last two days was to sleep. It seemed every waking hour Vintam had some activity planned for them. Usually while pressing her close to his side and flashing his charming smile at her, though she could do without both. Part of their activities involved welcoming the steady stream of nobility arriving for the impending event.

But most of their activities had to do with arrangements for the wedding ceremony, which left Esta a bit conflicted. Marriage was not a thought she'd often entertained, though part of her did find excitement in the idea and planning aspects of it.

Until she remembered it wasn't even her wedding. And her betrothed was a cold-hearted murderer she'd gladly have exchanged for her parents. Then, it didn't matter where the vase of flowers stood or when each course of the meal would be served. All of it was a sham, and Vintam went about it, oblivious that she was about to ruin more than just his wedding day. And Esta was perfectly content with that.

"Oh," she said, spotting Vintam's blond hair near the far wall. He walked with another man in dark clothing, and a seriousness hung over both of them. The man opened the gilded door to the hallway, and a silvery-blue glint on his finger caught the light of the chandeliers. Esta's breath caught. *The bad man.*

She set her glass down on a nearby table. "Excuse me for a moment." She curtsied to Lady Evie, who simply dipped her head and strolled off towards another group.

Esta wound her way across the marble tiles through the shifting mass of nobles, flinching each time one of them bumped her exposed arms or the back of her stiff, cream-colored dress. The din of conversation and the smell of wine in the air made her nauseous. It was like walking through Gann's estate all over again. Only here, at least the men had sense enough to look at her respectfully, thanks to Vintam's reputation.

Esta cracked open the door just as Vintam and the man turned the corner at the far end of the corridor. Slipping away from the light and sound of the banquet hall, she crept after them, following the indistinct murmur of their echoing voices. After another turn, a door creaked open, and Esta peered around the wall in time to see them disappear into Vintam's study next to the library. She snuck to the door, holding her breath with each step of her obnoxious, heeled shoes. Esta pushed back a loose strand of her hair and pressed an ear to the painted surface.

"...important enough for you to show up in the middle of a court function?" said Vintam with a hint of a snarl. "Damn it, man! There are procedures for contacting me unannounced, and Tibris demands you adhere to them unequivocally. Your little stunt nearly put this entire enterprise at risk."

"Archon Tibris sent me himself," replied a deep voice. "I was not to tarry over the court's sensibilities."

Esta heard Vintam scoff. "Well, you certainly saw to that. What then justifies such a disruption?"

"Your intruders in the western forest. Archmage Savos noted his concern to the archon at the evidence of them on your hunt."

Esta's heart stopped.

"Savos is paranoid, even in his own castle."

"Then have the spies been accounted for, or shall I dispose of them?"

No! Rivan. Medin. She had to warn them, had to do something...

"No," said Vintam harshly. "I do not need an Imperial Silencer roaming the grounds on a ghost chase. I am fully aware of what occurs at Giltcrest, and these bandits—not *spies,* mind you—have already been addressed. They fled the moment my men entered the woods."

She almost sighed in relief. *They're safe. Thank Elowë.*

"Patrols along the western border have been doubled. And the vagabonds haven't been seen, nor any evidence found since.

Tibris placed this project under my care," Vintam snarled. "I suggest you let me handle my own affairs."

"If you are so perceptive of Giltcrest's activities, then are you aware one of your guests is now at the door?"

Esta gasped. She stepped back as boots stomped towards her. There was nowhere to run. Instinctively, she raised her hand as if to knock.

Vintam flung open the door, wrath painted on his face. For a moment, surprise wiped it away, before his typical, charmed politeness asserted itself. Though a hint of coldness played at the edge of his tone.

"Isla, my dear," he said. "What are you...?"

"My–my apologies, I..." she stammered. "I noticed you had disappeared. I was concerned."

"Disappeared?" Vintam frowned and stepped into the hall, pulling the door partly closed.

Esta took a step back. "It–it's just. It is almost time for the musicians to begin, and..."

"Ah." Vintam's expression relaxed, and he grinned. "How could I forget?"

"Will you dance with me?" Esta forced every ounce of eagerness she could muster from her fraying nerves.

"It is to my shame that I have made *you* request it." Vintam extended his arm for her to take. This time, she did so almost gratefully. He glanced at the dark man standing in the study. "You can relay my confirmation to our friend. Thank you for coming." Then, Vintam strode down the hall, pulling Esta with him. She could still feel the other man's brooding stare, chasing her through the bright, gilded corridors towards the banquet hall.

A Silencer. A real Imperial Silencer! She shivered. She'd heard stories of the archon's assassins and hidden agents. Ordans blamed them for pretty much anything that went wrong. It didn't help that they were the most powerful mages in Aldaria.

The rumors must be true, she thought as Vintam led her on. *He could actually* sense *me*. Even after months with Artis, it was clear she still had so much to learn about magic.

"Are you alright, my dear?" Vintam studied her with concern.

Esta shook the dread from her thoughts and smiled. "I am with you. How could I not be?"

Vintam beamed again, pulling her closer to his side. As he opened the door to the crowded room, the sound of music spilled into the hall. The nobles had shuffled towards the walls, leaving space where several couples had already begun moving to the emptied center.

Vintam stretched out his hand. "Shall we?" Esta nodded, and he led her to join the other dancers.

Her back stiffened as his arm wrapped around her, his other hand holding hers carefully but firmly. Her feet stepped with his as they danced across the polished marble, her soft dress flowing around her. Vintam's eyes never left her, burning with that quiet intensity that her instincts feared more than the Silencer prowling the manor halls. She looked away from his gaze, glimpsing the other nobles, most of them watching her as she and Vintam flowed across the room. She saw Comtesse Mirabelle, the woman's gray eyes gleaming as she marked their dance.

"Do they unsettle you?" asked Vintam in a low voice.

She focused back on him. "No, just unfamiliar."

He smiled as they twirled. "They see your beauty and your grace. How you have so quickly won your way into my heart and their court. There is a power in your spirit, Isla. They sense your quiet fierceness, as I have. And they are a court that craves power."

Her chest tightened as he spun her, bringing her back into his arms. "Should I be concerned?"

He chuckled. "It is the Imperial court. You should always be concerned. But let them see you. And let them fear a power they will never have."

She nodded, letting him lead and enduring the feel of his hands against her until the song ended and the dancers took their bows and curtsies. Vintam kissed her hand and stepped back, relinquishing his hold on her.

"Excuse me for a moment, my dear," he said with another charming smile. "There is something I need to discuss with Archmage Savos while he is unoccupied."

Esta dipped her head, and he vanished into the throng of onlookers as new partners made their way onto the floor.

"You looked lovely out there." Esta jumped as Lady Morven appeared beside her.

"Oh, why, thank you."

Morven stared at the dancers, and Esta followed her gaze until she found the man it was fixed upon. Whom she took to be Lord Trevan, leaping across the floor with a pretty woman beaming in his arms.

"Sometimes, I wonder if I would have been better off marrying outside of the archon's council," said Morven. Her face and tone were somber, and a faint glint of longing hung in her expression. "Not that my father would have allowed it. But maybe life would have been simpler without all of the magic and conniving and secrets."

A twinge of sympathy filled Esta. "I'm sorry, Lady Morven."

She shook her head. "Just remember what you are getting into, Isla. Even Giltcrest is not as safe as it seems." Morven turned and disappeared into the crowd.

Esta watched as the dancers twirled around the room and laughter echoed over the music. Morven was right—in more ways than she knew. The archon's nobles played their game with secrets, lies, and hidden dangers. And Esta had walked into all of it willingly. She knew surviving Medin's mission was a challenge in itself. She only prayed she'd outlast the deadly, smiling faces in the room long enough to complete it.

⎯⎯◆◯◆⎯⎯

A soft rap on the door startled her. Esta grabbed the dusky robe off her bed to cover her shift, then cracked the door. "Jack?"

The boy looked nervously down the hall, shifting his feet. "Can you come to the hideout?"

Esta shook her head. "Everyone is retiring for the night. It's too risky. You need to go!"

Laughter echoed from the hallway, and Jack froze. Esta swung the door wider.

"In!"

Jack scurried into her room, and she locked the door, silently thanking Elowë her chambermaid had already left for the night.

"What are you doing here?" she whispered. "You know this isn't a good time."

He bobbed his shaggy head. "I know, but it's important. I found something."

"Okay." Esta gestured to the seats in the sitting room.

Jack gawked at the gilded furniture, running his hand across the white, luxurious cushion of the couch. "Your room's amazing."

"Your hideout is better." Esta smirked, taking a seat in the chair next to him. "So, what did you find?"

He hopped onto the couch, his small legs dangling from the deep seat. His face turned serious. "I saw some men taking things through the servants' entrance. Stuff not for the party."

"What kind of things?"

"Crates, mostly. Big ones, and funny-shaped ones. They took them down to the wine cellars."

Esta raised a brow. "Isn't that where crates of wine are usually taken?"

"I know what wine crates look like," he said defensively. "These were definitely not them. And when I tried to follow the men into the cellars, they were gone."

"Like they'd already left?"

Jack shook his head. "No. They didn't come back up at all. I got nervous and went back to the kitchens. I waited there for over an hour. I think Cook got tired of me hanging around. But no one came back through from the cellars."

"Hmm. There must be another way out. A way Vintam has kept hidden..."

Excitement ran through Esta. *Finally. A lead.*

"Jack, I can't thank you enough. This is exactly what I need." She stood and began pacing. "Now, I just need to signal—" Esta froze. The forest. Vintam's soldiers had forced Rivan and the others to retreat. And her wandering the forest edge with his new patrols would only end in her being caught. How in Aldaria would she reach them now? She cursed under her breath.

"What's wrong? What signal?" asked Jack with a worried look.

Esta sighed. "I was supposed to let my friends know once I knew where the secrets were being kept, so we could stop them. But Vintam's men chased my friends away."

"Are *they* the people in the woods?"

"Yeah, they were." Esta bit her lip, staring at the dark grounds beyond her window.

"They're still there."

She swerved to face him. "*What*?"

"Addi said she just saw one yesterday, but he disappeared really fast. The grownups think we're just making up stories now."

"Tell me everything, please." Esta sat down on the edge of her seat.

"There's a few of the other kids who aren't too bad," said Jack, kicking his legs. "As long as Claude and Braxton aren't around and we get our chores done, sometimes we go exploring in the woods."

"And the guards don't stop you?"

Jack shrugged. "I don't think they really care what we do, as long as we stay out of the way. But Addi showed me this afternoon where she saw him, and I even found an old footprint! I can usually find more than she can."

Esta's mind raced. If Rivan and the others were still close by, and Jack could reach them, then there was still a chance. But they'd never make it across the estate grounds with the extra patrols. She needed another way.

"Jack," she said thoughtfully, "how many deliveries does Giltcrest receive each day?"

"Um, normally, maybe one or two. But there's at least three with the wedding and archon's court here."

"Are they always the same people? Always to the same entrance?"

Jack shook his head. "There's been more faces than I can remember. But yes, even the strange men came to the servants' entry."

Esta tapped her chin and stood, then strode to the painted desk in the corner. After rummaging through the drawers, she found a stack of parchment, quills, and an inkwell. She scribbled furiously as Jack wandered over to her, curious. Once it had dried, she carefully folded the paper and passed it to him.

"You can read it if you want," said Esta. "But do you think you can get this to my friend, Rivan? I think I know how they can get in."

"I'll go to the forest first thing tomorrow! But... I–I can't read," Jack said bashfully, stowing the letter in his pocket. "Cook never taught me."

Esta's brows rose. Even Rivan had made sure she'd learned to read. After all, how else did you know what you were signing up for with every Thieves' Guild contract?

"Well. We'll just have to rectify that once we escape." She watched as he fidgeted. "You *have* thought about coming with me, right?"

"Yeah, and I think I want to. I'm just... scared." Jack lowered his head.

Esta bent to his level. "That's nothing to be ashamed of. I know what it's like to leave everything you've known. But Giltcrest isn't worthy of you, Jack. It's your cage, like the streets were mine. And there's a whole world waiting where you'll be free."

He looked up, excitement rising over his fear. "And I'll get to be with you. I hope I like where you live."

Esta laughed. "Well, it tends to be a bit hotter than here, but I think you'll enjoy it."

"Are you really from Araphon, then?"

"Well..." She grinned nervously. "A little farther south, actually. My home is in Caroca, in Orda."

"Orda!" Jack gasped. "But that's where wicked rebels live."

"Jack. You've lived at Giltcrest, in the Empire, your whole life. And now you've met me. One of those rebels, I suppose. Do you really think it's that simple?"

He cocked his head, thinking hard. "I, well... I guess maybe not. You're a lot nicer than the grownups say." His face reddened, and she placed a hand on his shoulder.

"I promise. You'll be safe with me in Orda. And once we're back at the palace, you can learn to read and make more friends and..." Esta stopped.

She could see it. She could imagine Attas chuckling as he welcomed Jack in the lofty throne room. Artis as she drilled him with lessons as she had Esta. He would even scowl at Artis like she had. Maybe Arano, the greatest swordsman she had ever met, would give Jack a mock duel with sticks from the gardens.

She could actually help give Jack hope, and she wanted desperately to do so. How had she grown to care about this boy so much this quickly?

"Wow. So, you're really a princess then?" Jack gaped at her as if he hadn't noticed her pause.

She smiled. "Not exactly. But what matters is there's a home for you there, a real home. If you'll come with me."

Jack nodded. "I will."

Esta pulled him into a hug, his small arms wrapping around her neck. She'd only ever hugged Rivan and her uncles like that. "Thank you."

He stepped back as she rose, blinking moisture away from her eyes.

"Now," she breathed. "We just have to get my friends into the estate and stop Vintam. Then we'll throw a party so big, Vintam's wedding will look like a funeral."

Jack beamed. "I'll find them. I promise."

They walked to the door, Esta cracking it to scan the hall. Everything was silent. She turned to him.

"Can you make it back to the servants' passage?"

"I'll go fast."

With a last sweep, she opened it, and Jack bolted for the hidden door. She watched as he pulled the line of gilded paneling to release the secret entry. He looked back, and after a small wave, darted out of sight.

Esta exhaled and slumped against the painted door.

He'd done it. Jack had found exactly what she needed, and she was one step closer to her mother's lost secrets. The next moment, realization nearly took her breath away.

It wasn't just that he was an echo of herself. She was meant to help Jack. Jack was meant to help her. They had met each other for a reason. And now, they each had hope. She tilted her face upwards. There wasn't another answer as to how all of it had been orchestrated so perfectly.

"Thank you," she whispered. Medin had been right. He'd been there all along. She only needed eyes to see him. Now she just needed to trust.

"Whatever happens, keep that boy safe."

Chapter 16
Out of Time

A LAUGH TORE ESTA'S gaze off the ripples of the pond and its reeds rustling in the warm, afternoon breeze. She pretended to smooth the sides of her slim, summer dress. Really, it was to wipe the sweat from her palms.

Today was it. Her last day before Prince Avaj, along with the *real* Isla, would arrive, and Esta's ruse would be discovered. The day she'd finally expose the secrets her parents had died for.

She swept the group of nobles mingling on the stone terrace overlooking the wide pond beyond the manor gardens. No sign of Jack yet. She sighed. *Surely they're in. They have to be by now.*

Esta climbed the stairs from the pond's grassy shore back onto the terrace with the others. As much as she hated all the smiling and niceties required to blend in with the archon's court, the last thing she could afford now was to draw attention. She already drew enough simply by being Lord Vintam's bride.

She walked to the edge of the group where the willows along the banks met the pines farther up the slope, casting their shadows onto the end of the terrace. Esta flashed her teeth at

Comtesse Mirabelle for good measure as she passed, the older woman locked in conversation with another lady Esta hadn't met yet. Esta picked up a fan from one of the scattered tables, pretending to cool herself as she looked again for the familiar mop of brown, boyish hair.

"Princess Isla," came a whisper. Esta jumped. Jack stood beside her as if he'd materialized out of the trees. "Your, um, delivery has arrived safely."

She nodded, suppressing her relief. "Thank you, Jack. Could you tell them I will be along shortly to... inspect it?"

"Yes, princess." Jack grinned and then scampered off towards the gardens.

As she faced the others once more, she spotted Comtesse Mirabelle daintily tracing a path through the crowd in her direction. Esta groaned inwardly. The last thing she wanted now was to be dragged into a conversation about another court scandal or the delays in imported furs from Terestia. Suddenly, the comtesse stopped.

"My dear, care to join me?"

Esta nearly flinched as Lord Vintam appeared at her side. He stretched out a hand, his dark eyes gleaming above a charming smile. Esta politely accepted, and he took her arm in his, leading her down to the little trail through the willows along the bank.

No, no, no! The other way. I need to get to the estate, not closer to him.

But Vintam had proved even more difficult than Mirabelle to shake. Esta was lucky Jack caught her when he did, in between endless introductions to other court lords and lying about how wonderfully excited she was for the ceremony as Vintam beamed beside her.

"Can you believe it has been a mere two weeks since your arrival at Giltcrest?" asked Vintam as they strolled along the simple dirt path. Willow branches pressed in around her, quickly shrouding them from the terrace. "It feels as if we have been together for years."

"It is hard to believe," answered Esta, "for such a short time."

Vintam pulled her arm closer, their bodies touching. Esta forced herself not to recoil. She hated when he did that. He looked at her softly. "I hope you will be happy here, with me." He brushed aside a mass of willow strands over the path, guiding them into the tree's obscuring cover.

Vintam pulled her closer to the wide trunk at its center, then turned to face her. "Are you happy, Isla?" He took her hands in his, stepping closer.

"Of course." Esta summoned a smile, resisting the urge to wrench out of his grasp.

His gaze bored into her, sweat trickling down her spine. He moved closer, their chests almost touching. Her pulse quickened. That intensity, that hunger, rose in his expression as he loomed over her.

"For your beauty, I will give you everything you have ever desired," he murmured. He took a step, backing her against the tree's rough bark. His hand slid up her bare arm. "Everything."

Vintam leaned forward, his face inches from her own, and her insides screamed.

Esta pushed on his chest, ducking away from his lips. "I, it–it isn't proper," she stammered, taking another step to the side. He moved closer.

"Would you deny your lord?" he asked playfully. He smiled, but the hardness in his eyes nearly petrified her.

Esta raised her hands. "There are only a few days left until the ceremony. We need only a little more patience."

He smirked, taking another step. "Patience is not something I am skilled at."

Her heart nearly beat out of her chest. She glanced at the rustling branchlets. "I–I feel rather warm in all this foliage." A laugh from the terrace whispered through the trees, and Esta inched towards it. "Please, let's rejoin the others."

Vintam moved closer, his gaze still burning. Esta wasn't sure she could fend him off, wrapped in all the willow branchlets and her dress, but it didn't mean she wouldn't try.

His eyes narrowed for the slightest of moments, and then he stopped and straightened. "Of course."

With a curt bow, he offered his arm. Tentatively, Esta took it, then he tugged her out of the entrapping leaves and into the light. A brooding silence hung between them, as heavy as the hot stillness of the air. She didn't dare look at him. His sharp movements and tightened arm gave her all the dread she could handle.

They burst from the trees and back into the warm sunlight along the water's edge. At the terrace steps, Vintam released her, giving another rigid bow. "Until later."

Esta curtsied shakily as he turned and strode toward another group of richly dressed men farther down the shore. Without another look, Esta clambered up the steps, breathing hard.

She needed to get out of here. Now.

She hurried towards the columns marking the path to the manor gardens.

"My dear, you look troubled." Lady Morven's voice froze her in her tracks. Esta shook the fear from her face as Morven shuffled closer and took her arm. Morven led her towards Comtesse

Mirabelle and Lady Katrin, chatting together by one of the tall, stone tables. Morven studied her as they joined the pair. "Is everything all right?"

"Yes, of course," said Esta. Her neck prickled, and she risked a glance to her side. Vintam's hard stare was fixed on her from across the terrace. She shivered.

"Why, she is simply dizzy with excitement!" said Mirabelle with a chuckle. "It is, after all, nearly the biggest day of her life. Don't you remember the feeling? The nerves?"

Esta gave a nervous laugh and nodded. Her mouth felt like cotton.

"Well, one could hardly blame her," said Lady Katrin. "The princess likely has several reasons to be anxious."

Esta peeked at him again. Vintam had turned away, engaged in conversation with Lord Trevan and several others.

"I–I'm sorry," she said. "Excuse me. I need some time to collect myself."

"Of course, my dear," said the comtesse, waving a hand. "You ought to prepare for the evening. Best foot forward, I always say. After all, there are few evenings left where you will be alone." Esta curtsied, masking a horrified shudder at the thought.

As calmly as she could, Esta walked to the exit, resisting the urge to look once more at Vintam. The moment she reached the short flight of steps to the manor gardens, she quickened her pace, focusing straight ahead on the pale, looming walls of the manor.

⊷⟡⊶

Esta shut the painted door, taking a deep breath. As lovely as her room was, she wasn't sorry it was the last time she would see it.

She patted the side of her dress where her pocket concealed the crystal ring. It seemed almost a shame that it alone would escape with her after all the effort Artis went through to assemble her wardrobe. But she doubted Vintam would allow her to fetch her luggage before racing back to Orda.

Orda.

Esta's heart leapt at the thought of home. To be back in her uncle's palace with its bright halls and the peaceful garden lake. Back with people who genuinely cared for her. She walked down the hall, excited thoughts of Rivan, Medin, and the others waiting for her displacing—for a moment—the worry brewing in her soul. Light streamed through the endless windows along the corridor to her left, shining off the marble floors and painted walls. She turned the corner.

"Going somewhere, my dear?"

She froze. Vintam stood with his arms crossed over his silk vest, smiling. She took a step back.

"I, I just—"

"Mirabelle insisted you simply needed time to prepare after our lengthy day," he said, strolling closer. "She said you looked quite flushed."

"I–I really ought to get dressed for this evening," Esta stammered, her chest pounding.

Vintam's gaze slowly climbed from her legs, lingering on each part of her. "You look beautiful the way you are." Her face reddened.

"Then the dress I have for this evening will be even more worth the wait." She turned to walk back towards her room. "It's best I—" His hand latched onto her wrist, catching her other arm as he pulled her to him.

He clicked his teeth. "Enough games, my dear. We have delayed our desire long enough."

Esta tugged against his hold, his iron grip dragging her so close she could feel the warmth of his breath. "I have agonized for months, waiting for your hand. And I have done my best to wait for your father and this blasted ceremony. But having you here these past weeks, alone with me, has only deepened my desire. As I said, patience is not a skill of mine."

He grinned as panic rose inside Esta, struggling against his strength. She yelped as he flung open the door beside them and hauled her into the room.

"Let go!"

He pressed her closer, putting his lips beside her ear, and whispered, "Everything will be yours, as you will be mine. Forget the rest. Give in to it."

His lips tickled her neck, and her panic turned into terror. Fear and instinct left only one choice. Esta reared her head, then flung it forward. Pain lanced across her temple as something cracked, and Vintam yelled. His grip on her arms loosened. With a moment of freedom, she swung her knee, landing an unladylike kick, even in her dress, and he groaned. His hold on her vanished. Bolting for the door, Esta frantically pushed a vase off a side table, sending it crashing towards Vintam as the table toppled over. She yanked the door shut, pulled up the end of her gown, and ran.

Esta sprinted down the hall, heedless of Vintam's ringing curses and the mess of hair whipping across her face. Bile rose in her, every ounce of her shaking and threatening to send her to the floor. *Rivan. Medin. Elowë, get me to them.*

She turned down another corridor. It wasn't familiar. *No. Did I take the left turn? Where are the stairs?!*

She kept running. Vintam's shouts rang behind her. More paintings and gilded trim flashed by as she ran. Esta swerved around another corner. A small figure startled her, and she nearly tripped.

"Es—Princess Isla!" Jack's eyes widened in shock.

"Jack. No time," said Esta, breathless. "The cellars. You've got to hide."

Behind them, Vintam yelled again. Closer.

Jack glanced past her. "Is he chasing you?"

She grabbed his arm, preparing to run again. "We've got to *move*."

The boy yanked free. "Esta, the bad men are here!"

"What?"

"Th—there are two of them at the door. I'm scared, but I'm going to be brave. I can help."

Esta shook her head frantically. "No! You need to get out of here *now*. It's too dangerous to stay at Giltcrest. Get as far away from Vintam as you can." She dropped beside him, her instincts screaming to run as she met his fear-filled eyes. "Go to Ilagron. I'll find you. Just, get somewhere safe, Jack. Promise me."

Jack nodded. "I promise."

Vintam's furious shout rang down the corridor.

Esta jumped to her feet. "Now, go. Get—"

"I promise I'll go *after* I help my friend."

Esta growled. "You—"

"There's a servants' passage around that corner." Jack pointed behind them. "The wall past the suit of armor. Take it all the way down and then right." He furrowed his little brow. "Now, *you* promise me. Go stop the bad men, and don't turn back."

"Jack—"

"Esta, go!"

A lump rose in her throat. She nodded, then turned and ran. Her heart and head raged inside her. How could she leave him? Was this mission worth sacrificing *Jack*? What made her any different from Vintam? What would happen to the world if she failed?

She ducked around the corner just as Vintam's rampant scowl rounded the other end. Esta sprinted past the armor, her hands slamming into the gilded paneling of the empty wall next to it. *Creator, where's the latch?*

"Fool boy! Out of my way!"

A length of panel shifted, and she pulled. The hidden door slid open without a sound. A slap echoed from the hall, and Jack shrieked. Esta stopped, rage boiling inside her. She turned back, but Jack's words rang in her head. He'd asked her to promise. And he'd sacrificed for her. With stinging tears, Esta retreated into the dark passage and shut the door.

Shame burned inside her as she felt along the wall, inching her way down the lightless stairs.

I left him. I left Jack.

She rubbed away the tears with her trembling hand. All she could see was Jack's giddy face, bobbing through the garden maze or handing her another treasure from his hideout. She felt like a traitor.

The stairs abruptly ended, and Esta nearly collided with a new wall in front of her. She ran her hand along the icy stone to her right, following the new path. After several minutes and a turn, a faint glimmer of light appeared near the floor ahead of her. Esta hurried forward, feeling along the sides of the wall for the release. Pulling the handle, the hidden door opened with a muted click, bathing her in a dim, blinding light. She blinked, wiping away more tears as she adjusted to the clammy room and barrels before her.

A young man with loose, black hair and brown skin stepped from behind a pillar, and Esta gasped.

"Rivan!"

Chapter 17
Trapped

Esta sobbed as she clung to Rivan, burying herself in his arms. He wrapped them around her tightly.

"Es. Sweet Elowë, I missed you." Rivan rested his chin on her head. "You had us worried sick!"

She stepped back, trembling. "Rivan, I left him. I left him. I didn't want to, but Vintam was coming and..."

Rivan put his hands on her shoulders. "Who, Es?"

"Jack. The boy," she said haltingly. "He–he made a distraction so I could escape, and I just *let* him!"

"Es." Medin's gentle voice pulled her gaze away. Her uncle stood beside her, relief and sadness mingling in his dark eyes.

Esta moved to him, letting Medin wrap her in a hug.

"We'll do what we can for him," he said, "but we've got to finish this and get the Empire's knowledge back to Orda. Before Vintam discovers us." Esta bit her lip and nodded.

"Hey, where's my hug?" asked Brunce, crossing his massive arms as he leaned against a stack of crates. Esta sniffled and rolled her eyes.

"Later," said Artis sternly across from him. "We need to move."

"Right." Medin gestured towards the far end of the wine cellar. "Over here. Esta, do you still have that crystal ring?"

She pulled it from her pocket, thankful it had survived her escape. Medin led her to a space between two towering shelves of wine crates. Had it been any other time, nothing about the wall would've been remarkable. But as her uncle stopped in front of it, the empty gap felt strangely out of place in a cellar perfectly maximized to store Vintam's collection.

"Remember what I said?" asked Medin, pointing at the wall. "I believe we've found its purpose."

Esta moved closer. There, level with the middle of her chest and off to one side, were four irregular grooves etched into one of the otherwise ordinary bricks. She ran a finger over the bumps of the ring's crystalline shard. She glanced at Medin.

He nodded. "You do the honors, Es."

She stepped forward, raising the silvery-blue crystal to the grooves. Carefully, she rotated the ring until the shard slid into the holes. A blue light flashed from the edges of the mortar, and she jumped. With a rumble, the wall slid open, revealing a passage trailing into darkness.

"Well done, my friends," murmured Arano behind her. "Medin, your theories and honor have been proven."

"We will see," he replied, gesturing for Artis to take the lead.

She stepped forward, summoning a small orb of light over her palm. Esta stared at her in amazement. The brief displays by the Imperial lords over the past two weeks had likewise enthralled her, even as she despised their decadent arrogance. Artis strode into the passage without a word, and the rest followed. Esta and Rivan brought up the rear, partly covered in darkness, as Brunce's hulking form blocked the orb's light.

Rivan nudged her as they walked, passing her a narrow, metal rod.

Not a rod. A sword.

Esta shot him a look, and Rivan shrugged.

"We smuggled them inside the crates. With so much going on for the party, the servants didn't even bother checking. Medin made sure there were enough, in case…"

Esta nodded, still trembling from her harrowing escape and now, the looming dangers. She gripped the small sword's hilt tighter, relieved to have some form of defense, even if it meant her cover as the princess was gone. Her lip quivered, thinking back to Jack and his last words. Tears threatened to rise again as his little yelp reverberated in her mind.

"Es, do you need to stop?" Rivan asked.

"No."

"You've been through a lot, I'm sure. If you need a moment—"

"Rivan, I'm fine. It's just… I feel horrible, leaving Jack like that. I should've stayed. I should've fought Vintam off."

Rivan placed a hand on her shoulder. "It sounds like he was really brave, and he wanted to help you."

"I know," she whispered. "And that's why I can't lose this chance. We have to finish this, for our parents, and now, for him."

"We will. Together."

Light grew ahead of them through a narrow archway until they all filed through, and Artis extinguished her orb. Esta blinked in the bright, unnatural light.

"Whoa…"

A massive, two-story chamber spread before her. From their vantage above, she could see across the rows of tables and shelves. Strange, iron chandeliers illuminated the perfectly carved stone of the walls and columns. Squinting, Esta noticed the lights of the chandeliers were glass spheres with balls of light inside rather than flames, unlike anything she had ever seen.

"There."

Esta looked at Medin as he pointed towards a group of tables at the far end of the room before another set of hallways which led farther into the complex. To their left, a long ramp sloped from their walkway down to the lower floor. They followed as her uncle led the way.

"Where are we?" Esta murmured, still scanning the room.

"The passage led away from Giltcrest," replied Artis, keeping pace beside her. "I expect we are somewhere underneath the gardens or field. And this chamber has been carved by magic."

Esta raised a brow. "Magic?"

"Can you not tell?" Artis sniffed. "It is too precise, the stone too clean. Curious, given Lord Vintam's stature. I wonder if it predates him."

"And all that?" Esta gestured to the tables and shelves. Faint gleams of silvery-blue dotted their surfaces between stacks of books, parchments, and metal instruments that reminded Esta of the devices alchemists in Caroca always had sitting about.

"The source of our problems and the key to our answers."

Esta eyed the foreboding passages leading from the main room. "It's too quiet. What if there are others down here?"

"We keep our eyes and ears open," said Artis. "So far, I do not sense another presence nearby."

They paused as Medin came to a stop before the sprawling workstations. He turned to the group.

"Spread out, and find anything you can," he said. "Ignore the shards for now. We need to know what they are and what the Empire is planning to do with them."

As the others hurried into the maze, Esta turned to Brunce. "Want to come with me?"

"I'd only get in the way," he grunted. "Leave the searching to the others."

She smirked. "You don't sound like much of a spy."

"I'm not here to spy."

"Then why *are* you here?" Esta put a hand on her hip.

Brunce grinned, wrinkling his scars. "I'm Plan B."

"Plan B?"

"The part where we punch our way out." He cracked his knuckles, then tugged at the straps of his steel battle gloves. "You help, little bird. I'll keep watch."

Esta nodded and hurried towards the others. Arano spotted her from a line of tables littered with small crystals and loose papers.

"Ah, Lady Esta," he said, "the far end of this row looks promising, if you would."

"Sure." Esta walked to the table at the opposite end, sifting through scribbles and half-filled journals. She stopped on one page, a sketch of one short, multi-pronged shard suspended atop the table by clamps in a metallic stand in front of her.

"Hmm, 'iluvan.'"

"What was that?" called Arano.

Esta looked up. "Here." She waved the paper, drawing Medin's gaze as well. "The crystals. They're called iluvan."

Medin circled around to her. "What else does it say?"

Esta scanned the paper, grabbing the others from its pile. "It talks about how the shards possess magical power, to varying degrees. Unlike anything the Empire has found before. Their mages can sense it, but only a few have been able to access its energy."

Medin looked at Artis in the next row. "Artis?"

The mage picked up one of the small iluvan shards on her table, its surface sparkling in the light. "I feel its power, but more as if from a distance. Its energy is... shrouded."

"What do you mean?" asked Esta.

Artis sighed. "It is difficult to explain. But I do not think I can connect to it. These shards are truly unique. I confess I am as lost as the rest of you. Does it say where the Empire discovered them?"

Esta flipped through the pages again. "No."

"Here!" Rivan called from across the room. The group hurried over, huddling around a desk with a set of iluvan and a thick, leather-bound journal.

"These are entries from some kind of head researcher," Rivan explained, tapping the open journal. "A mage summarizing findings to report to Vintam."

"Perhaps someone you saw?" Medin asked, looking at Esta.

She shook her head. "I don't think so. The only mages I saw were members of the archon's court. Well, other than the Silencer."

"Silencer?" Medin's stare hardened.

"He—he was here several days ago and confronted Vintam about your presence in the woods. Vintam dismissed him, though. Vintam said he'd taken care of everything."

"Well, quite the arrogant Imperial, isn't he?" said Arano dryly.

"Listen," said Rivan, drumming the journal again. "The researcher mentioned a shipment of iluvan arriving from an excavation site. The shards, in his words, 'bear a striking re-semblance to the iluvan deposits recovered from Elvish sites in Fellinor and from the first expedition to'"—Rivan scrunched his face—"to 'the lost world.'"

"Lost world?" Medin echoed. "What lost world?"

Rivan shrugged. "'Dunno. It doesn't say anything further about it."

The group looked at each other in confusion.

"So... they found iluvan somewhere else, but then also in Fellinor," said Esta, rubbing her temples. "Why? They must have a reason for—"

"Yes," Rivan interrupted. "Here it is. Oh, how did we miss that? It's literally right above us."

Esta tilted her head up.

"The lights," explained Rivan. "They figured out a small-scale way to use the iluvan's power as a source of energy. Their first success was in creating light."

Artis' eyes widened. "Impossible. Devices that are pow-ered by magic?"

Esta gestured upwards. "It's kind of hard to argue, though."

Medin turned back to her brother. "The Empire won't stop with chandeliers."

"No." Rivan flipped to another page. "There are a lot of failed experiments mentioned here. A few explosions. I bet that was interesting. And... Oh."

"What?"

"There's something about replicating the 'discovery.' Creat-ing a prototype." Rivan swallowed. "The mage, and Vintam, appear to believe recreating it—whatever *it* is—is the key to doing more. There are some vague theories about new weapons, defenses… more. Any invention the Empire can dream of, powered by this new magic."

"With that kind of power, Orda wouldn't stand a chance," Esta muttered.

"If this discovery is a weapon, we need to find it," said Medin.

Rivan nodded, scanning more of the journal. "The mage requested some 'expedition logs' be brought to another chamber here to help map out the device's design."

"Then it's close." Medin turned to Esta. "Es, go with Artis and see—"

"Company!" Brunce hollered from across the room.

Esta turned with the others to face the balcony they'd entered from as clanging boots rang from its darkened opening. She gripped her small sword tighter as a dozen Imperial soldiers marched into the room, spreading along the wall. Archers at the ends of the balcony raised their bows, deadly arrows pointed at her and the others, who edged closer to the shelves and columns nearest them.

Esta's breath caught as Lord Vintam strode to the rail, his dark eyes blazing. She shivered as he lingered on her before glancing at the others.

"Well. It took you fool Ordans long enough to figure out a way in," said Vintam with a sneer. "Now we can finally end this ridiculous charade."

Her stomach dropped. *He knew.*

"Surprised?" Vintam chuckled. "Archon Tibris has known about Orda's meddling for months. All that time, he and I have been orchestrating this, knowing you would take the bait."

"You risked exposing your secrets?" asked Medin, stepping forward.

"Tibris would have rather his Silencers finished you in the woods. But Giltcrest is *mine*, and so is the glory of ending you myself." Vintam pointed a finger at him. "I didn't need to see your face to know who you are, Lord of the Ashguard. I hope you aren't here for some vain notion of revenge."

"Revenge would be far simpler, wouldn't it?" said her uncle quietly.

"That woman should never have come here. She paid the price for her trespass, and you are a fool to follow in her footsteps."

Esta clenched her fist. "How dare you!"

Vintam looked at her with disgust. "Ah, yes. *You*." He glanced at Medin. "The girl was a clever ruse. She is just as deserving of the praise of Princess Isla's beauty." He turned back to Esta. "A pity you did not take my offer to forget it all. You would have made a fine mistress."

"Never. You murdered my mother and father, you monster," Esta hissed, raising her blade.

Vintam's brows raised. "Mother? Then you... I must say, that *is* unexpected." He huffed. "Well done. I am rarely taken aback. Even so, it is rather convenient that all of my loose ends are right here in front of me."

She took a step, fury blazing in her eyes. "What did you do to Jack?"

"The urchin boy?" Vintam scoffed. "Stupid child. I will deal with him later. Hopefully, he will still be useful once I am finished."

Fear and wrath raged inside her. "You won't get a chance."

Vintam laughed. "Bold words for a dead woman."

He flicked a hand.

Arrows flew from the archers on the balcony. Esta flinched, and the floor rumbled.

Thunk.

She opened her eyes. A wall of earth stood between her group and the soldiers, the din of steel and boots ringing off the stone chamber as they surged towards the ramp. With her arms still raised, Artis leapt from the cover of the earthen wall, flicking a hand at the archers. Gleaming shards of ice shot from her fingers. An archer gasped, falling against the rail as an icy bolt struck his chest. Another toppled back as ice sliced through his shoulder.

From the other end of the chamber, Brunce bellowed, charging from behind an overturned table at the mass of soldiers storming down the ramp.

"Artis! Far corner!" Medin shouted as more arrows pelted the rock. She launched another volley at a pair of archers.

"Lower hall!" Rivan pointed at the hallway behind them, and Esta's gut twisted.

More of them.

A fire sprang from the darkened hall.

"Mages!"

The fireball shot towards her, and Esta lunged. She felt the heat as flames sped past, colliding with a shelf and sending papers and instruments flying.

"Kill them!" Vintam screamed over the chaos.

She turned just in time to duck as the mage shot again. Then, the man suddenly grunted and fell. Rivan stood behind him, his sword gleaming as he panted.

"Thanks."

"Come on!" Rivan pointed towards Artis and Arano, locked in battle with more of Vintam's men pouring from the hall.

Esta spotted Medin and Brunce, lashing at a sea of armored swordsmen near the ramp. Vintam was nowhere to be seen. She charged a mage unleashing a barrage of ice at Artis, who ducked behind another wall of rock. Esta's blade sank into the man's back, and he fell, nearly taking her with him as she stumbled in her fraying dress. She scrambled back, feeling sick as she stared at the crumpled form before her.

She'd killed a man.

Esta had brawled with plenty of scoundrels and beaten several senseless. But she'd never killed. And never even seen a battle like this. She stared at the carnage around her. The charred, burning tables, bodies sprawled on the stone. *Elowë, not like this.*

"Esta!" Rivan roared over the noise. She snapped back just as Arano caught another soldier in front of her, parrying a blow and landing his own across the man's chest before she'd even blinked. Arano swerved to face her, his long hair flying around his eager face.

"Not now, my dear! Wits about you. Keep close!"

He turned as another pair of swordsmen rushed them. Arano stepped in front of her, raising his narrow sword.

"My good men, do you know who I am?"

"A dead man," one of them growled.

"*I* am Arano Deshad, the greatest swordsman you shall ever meet." Arano twirled his sword. "Prepare to die."

Like lightning, he struck, felling the first man before he could even react. The second swung; his sword smacked away as if it were no more than a nagging fly. Arano's blade flashed, and the second man collapsed in a silent heap.

"Come!"

Esta ran after him to where Rivan and Artis had pinned the last pair of mages in a corner. A gust of fire from a mage sailed over their heads, deflected by a blast from Artis. A bolt of energy shot from her hand, blasting the man into the wall behind him before he toppled onto the floor, lifeless.

The second mage shot a bolt of ice at Rivan, and he ducked. The man lunged, a dagger poised in his hand. Arano was on him in an instant, knocking the dagger from the mage's grip. Arano's blade cut through his robe, and the mage crumpled.

Rivan stumbled back, panting. "I owe you one."

Arano grinned. "Three, actually."

CHAPTER 18
SACRIFICE

ESTA STRUGGLED FOR BREATH, her mind reeling as she scanned the room. The hallway was clear, but Brunce and her uncle...

"Quickly! The ramp!" said Artis.

The swarm of soldiers had pushed Brunce and Medin back towards the rows of tables, men trying to flank past Medin's jabs and Brunce's lumbering swings to surround them. Esta watched in fascinated horror as Brunce caught a man's sword in his steel glove, snapping it in two before picking the man up by his breastplate. The massive brawler punched the soldier so hard that the force dented his chest and sent him careening into the row of men behind him.

"Reinforcements!" Arano shouted before racing into the fray.

Esta looked up to see more soldiers pouring from the cellar hallway.

"Back!" Medin yelled across the fray. "Make for the hall-way!"

The hallway. Jack had said that the men who came in never left. *It could be the other way out!*

"Come on!" said Esta, racing for the darkened passage.

"Medin!"

She froze as Artis cried above the shouts and clash of steel. At the center of the ravaged chamber stood her uncle, locked in a duel with Lord Vintam. More soldiers swarmed between them, pushing her and their group back.

"Uncle!" Esta raced towards them.

Brunce roared, launching another man through the air as an icy blast from Artis shot through a line of soldiers. Esta could see Medin's blade clashing against Vintam's own, the Imperial lord scowling as his loose sleeves whipped through the air. Esta flinched as Vintam's blow rang against Medin's sword. She had to reach him. Now.

She sprinted for the edge of the soldiers hemming them in, using Arano's whirlwind of strikes as cover. The last soldier's gaze flicked towards her, and she sprang. Her sword plunged into his gut and he gasped, stumbling back as her force carried them to the ground. She rolled off as others turned from Arano to surround her. Suddenly, Rivan was beside her, lashing out with his sword and driving the soldiers back. Esta glanced at Medin.

Vintam lunged, and her uncle parried, nicking the lord's arm as his momentum carried him forward. Vintam yelped, his face burning with anger, and pulled back. Medin jabbed, pushing Vintam back another step. Suddenly, her uncle froze, his shoulders trembling.

"No!" Esta screamed. She scrambled to her feet.

Vintam struck, but Medin swiped away the blade as his back hunched and writhed. Esta screamed again, bashing against a soldier's sword. Medin's arm shook violently, and Vintam hammered another blow, knocking the weapon from his hand.

Vintam stepped forward and plunged the blade into Medin's chest.

Esta's heart stopped.

Her uncle sank to his knees as Vintam towered over him, his teeth gleaming.

"*Medin!*"

Esta pounded against the soldier in front of her, heedless of anything but her uncle, sprawled on the floor. A blast of ice shot through the crowd, men shrieking as others shrank back. Rivan and Brunce roared beside her, charging the enemy ranks as Arano shouted over the ringing steel and Artis' blasts.

A wall of rock erupted from the floor around Medin, sending soldiers scrambling for cover as Esta's group converged on his fallen form. Vintam had vanished into the swarming soldiers once more. She stumbled beside her uncle, tears running through the grime on her cheeks.

"Uncle…"

Medin's breathing was shallow, and blood oozed from his side, pooling on the stone. His eyes fluttered open, resting on her with pain-filled pride.

"Es."

She took his hand, trembling as his warm fingers weakly clasped hers.

"Y–you can't," she choked. "We, we'll get you out of here. We—"

"Esta." Medin's tender gaze looked up at her. "It's up to you. Finish what Lara started. Protect… our people."

Esta shook her head, tears spilling across her tattered dress as her words came in gasps. "No. I, I can't lose you. Not–not now."

"Es—"

"We're supposed to go home. Together…"

Medin squeezed her hand. "I'm sorry, Es."

"No, Medin—" Her chest shook, a lump filling her throat.

"Trust him," rasped Medin. "It's not the end, only… the beginning. Trust… Elowë has a plan." He struggled for air, his grip loosening. "I'm so proud of you, Es. I love you."

"No. No, Medin—"

He sighed, and she felt life vanish from his body.

Esta wept. She lay across his chest, clinging to him as sobs wracked her body.

Medin was gone.

The uncle who had given her a home, had given her a family, had loved her, was gone.

Elowë, it wasn't supposed to end like this.

She'd barely found her family, and already it had been torn from her.

"Es…"

Rivan's gentle hand met her shoulder, his eyes brimming with tears.

"Esta, we have to go."

"Rivan," she said, gulping for air. "Rivan, he—"

"I know. But he asked us to go. We have to finish this. For all of them."

Esta rose, wiping her cheeks as she gazed at her uncle one last time. "For my parents. For you," she whispered.

Rivan helped her to her feet, and the chaos of battle tore into her world beyond the shelter of the wall.

"Go!" Artis yelled, nodding towards the hallway. "We'll cover you!"

"*What?*" Esta shrieked, still shaking. "No! We go together!" She looked in horror at the stream of soldiers charging down the ramp.

"No time, little bird!" Brunce bellowed, punching back another armored man with his steel battle glove. "Make Vintam pay!"

She swerved to Rivan. "We can't—"

"Come on." Rivan tugged her forward. "We have to move—now!"

A fireball smashed into the remains of a table beside them.

With her hand firmly in his, Rivan pulled her towards the hall. Esta ducked as more fireballs and arrows whistled past. They sprinted into the corridor, a blast narrowly missing Esta's heel. She turned, Artis meeting her gaze with a soft, proud smile. Then, the mage flicked her wrist.

Arano stepped beside Brunce, raising his sword as a line of soldiers charged. "I am Arano Deshad, the greatest swordsman you shall ever—"

Earth slammed shut against the ceiling, closing them in complete darkness and silence.

Esta's heart pounded against her ribs. Every part of her ached as she stared into the blackness.

Why? Why had Artis sealed them in?

Rivan's hand reached for hers in the dark. "Come on, Es," he murmured. "We have to find that research."

"Rivan," she said, her voice cracking as they felt their way forward. "Th–they're going to die. All of them are going to die if we don't help!"

His grip tightened. "We all will unless we find Vintam's secret. They knew what they were doing, Es. We have to make it count."

Esta forced down another sob.

So much pain. So much death.

For what? Some stupid crystals? Had her parents, her uncle, and now, her friends sacrificed everything for something so insignificant?

Vintam's victorious sneer flashed in her mind. His words rang in her ears.

They are a court that craves power.

No.

The iluvan was power. Unlimited power. The lords of the Hamid Empire already wielded their might with cruelty and arrogance. She'd seen it up close, had lived in their world. Amplified by the magic of these shards... Orda would fall. Aldaria would fall.

Rivan was right. Medin and her parents hadn't died to give up now. Elowë hadn't put her here to give up now.

"We'll stop him," she said, gripping Rivan's hand.

"We're in this together, Es, until the end. No matter what."

"No matter what."

After feeling their way to the end of the hall, they turned a corner. A faint light emanated from the distance, spilling into the dark. Cautiously, Esta and Rivan crept closer. Esta blinked as the light grew stronger. Rivan paused at the doorway, peeking around the edge with his sword against his chest.

"Clear."

Together, they stepped into the slowly pulsing light. A small room with bookshelves, a desk, and more metallic contraptions than Esta could count waited in the stillness beneath another of the strange iluvan fixtures. Stacks of ancient parchments and scattered iluvan littered the desk and shelves, adding to the chaos. Her gaze stopped on a blocky object at the far end, draped in a dusky tarp. Rivan strode across the room and yanked the cloth away.

"What in Aldaria...?"

Esta stared in confusion. An obelisk of white, polished stone sat beneath, larger than her and Rivan combined. The inside was hollow, a mess of spindly wires crisscrossing its innards and disappearing into holes formed in the sides. More metal strands poked from an open panel near its base, sprawling from behind a set of thick, golden brackets. As unkempt as the device was, there was a precision to the stonework Esta could only attribute to magic.

"What is this?" said Rivan.

"I have no idea. The prototype?"

"Maybe, but it's a mess. There's no way it's finished." Her brother glanced at the doorway. "Check the mage's desk. Maybe there's an answer. I'll keep watch."

Esta scurried to the paper-strewn desk as Rivan peered into the dark corridor. She laid her sword on its edge and shoved aside scraps detailing more iluvan shipments and scribbles, studying a couple that could have been pieces of the device. Or maybe just a chest and candlestick. She wasn't sure.

She shifted another stack of parchment, then paused. A worn, leather-bound book wrapped in a red ribbon sat beneath, tied with a gold clasp of a wolf's head, glaring at her. The seal of the Hamid Empire.

"Here's something," she murmured.

Rivan looked back. "Well?"

Carefully, Esta undid the clasp and drew back the ribbon. The weathered pages crinkled ominously as she opened the book.

She gasped. "It—it's the log. It reads, 'The Account of Captain Thranar Concerning the First Imperial Expedition to the Lost World. Recorded upon his return in the four-hundred and seventieth year of our Beneficent Lord's Glorious Rule.'"

"Four-hundred and seventy?" Rivan repeated. "That was over forty years ago. What's it got to do with now?"

Esta turned the pages as gently as she could. "It, it's so much. It talks about a ship and passage across the Endless Ocean. A way through to an unknown world. Rivan, there are sketches of ruins they found, unlike anything I've ever seen. They're beautiful."

"What else?"

"Here." She paused on a page with fading ink. "Something about excavating a chamber within the ruins. They found... I'm not sure, but there's something referred to as 'the pod.' And a man. Wait... A man *inside* the pod, maybe? It's too faded."

A rumble echoed through the corridor. "Es, hurry!"

Her dark hair swirled as she scanned the pages, and her heart beat faster.

"They took the pod," she continued, "but something happened. Something to the crew. They started going mad, raving about a voice in their heads. There was a thick fog. Some of them... Some of them fell dead where they stood. The last thing the captain saw was the pale fog blanketing the ruins." She flipped to the final pages. "Nothing else about the lost world. It says they brought the pod to Hamidia for study. And it mentions a bright, white crystal concealed at its base. They believed it was some kind of key but didn't want to remove it and risk destroying the device."

"An iluvan?" Rivan asked.

"Maybe."

Another rumble shook the room, louder.

"What are they doing? What's the Empire's plan?" Rivan demanded.

"I'm looking!" Esta grabbed another book from the back of the desk beside a long shard of iluvan, a book that appeared newer. She flipped it open.

"The head researcher's journal," she said triumphantly. Her eyes tore across the pages. A muffled clatter rose from the darkness. "Okay. The archon tasked Vintam with discovering how the pod worked. It sounds like he's one in a long line of researchers. Then something about not getting the connection to the iluvan right. Something is off with the design. But they're also trying to alter it somehow... 'amplify the barrier properties.' What does that mean?"

"It's a weapon," said Rivan quickly, turning towards her. "Whatever they found, they're creating a weapon."

"It's 'unstable,'" Esta read. She shook her head. "The Empire is missing something important. Nearly caved in this facility, it sounds like. His last note reads, 'Do not introduce iluvan into the conduit until the flaw is identified.'"

Esta glanced at the half-assembled device in the corner, drawn to the exposed golden brackets at the front. Their arms *did* appear to be missing something.

Suddenly, Rivan yelped. Esta turned.

Vintam sneered in the doorway as he held a dagger to Rivan's throat, gripping her brother in front of him. A scream lodged in her chest.

"Well, you *are* resourceful, aren't you?" Vintam said. "I should have eliminated you sooner."

Esta swiped her sword from the desk and took a step, fear pounding beneath her fury. "I'll kill—"

"Ah, ah." Vintam pressed the blade's tip into Rivan's skin. "Surrender, my dear. Unless you want his blood on your hands, too."

Esta gritted her teeth, gripping the sword hilt until her knuckles whitened. She wanted to plunge it into Vintam's arrogant chest, but Rivan...

With a shudder, she let it fall, clattering to the floor. She hated herself. Hated how helpless she felt as Vintam's expression turned to glee. She stared at her brother, tears forming in the corners of her eyes as she trembled with anger.

Rivan looked back. Not with fear, but smiling. The same smile he always wore after she'd returned home with a hard-earned loaf of bread. The smile after she'd won back their savings in a game of chance. The smile he'd worn holding her as a little girl, Esta quivering while a storm rolled over their hideout. The one she knew meant he would never leave her.

"Es," he gulped under Vintam's grip. "I love you. *Run!*"

Rivan shoved against Vintam, dislodging the arm holding him in place. He reached for Vintam's wrist as the lord yelled. Esta dropped, lunging for her blade and grabbing a pointed iluvan shard on the floor beside it. She stood, ready to charge Vintam.

When his dagger sank into Rivan's stomach.

"*Rivan!*" Esta screamed.

Her brother groaned, collapsing at Vintam's feet. Rage burned inside her, and she stomped forward. Two dark shapes rose from the gloom behind Vintam, their black robes emerging from the hall. She froze, dread seizing her.

Imperial Silencers.

Vintam panted and staggered back, shooting a venomous look at Rivan shuddering on the floor. Blood seeped through

Rivan's shirt as he moaned. Esta looked at him, caught between rage and terror.

Vintam pointed his dagger at her, fury blazing in his eyes. "Fool."

Esta barely noticed him. All she could see was Rivan, trembling before her as life bled from his body. She dropped her sword, tears falling down her cheeks.

"Please," she cried, looking helplessly at Vintam and the dark mages beside him. "You can save him. Please, just stop, and let him live."

"Let him live?" he mocked. He laughed, a wicked, evil laugh. "Fool girl. You have no idea what you're involved in."

Esta shrank back, watching Rivan squirm as Vintam stepped beside him.

"Your prize is long gone. Far out of Orda's reach," Vintam crowed. "You have *lost*."

"He's *dying*." She tore her gaze away as Vintam's gleeful sneer resumed.

"Archon Tibris let me choose. Did you know?" He chuckled. "Even without magic, I have his full confidence. And so, I sent the relic as far as possible from Orda and its filthy Ashguard. As a favor to a friend of mine in Starkhaven, actually. I have what I need from it, but perhaps it will give him something to do as he settles in on barbaric Karthmoor."

"Please," she croaked. The iluvan in her hand quaked as Rivan's gasps grew feebler, his shudders slowing.

"But you?" Vintam hissed, moving closer. "You're nothing but a scared, abandoned little girl. As pathetic as that urchin. Your life is mine."

Jack.

Esta glanced at Rivan again. Vintam had taken her parents. He'd taken her uncle. He'd take her brother. He wouldn't take Jack. *I have to end it all.* She gripped the thin iluvan shard tighter.

Vintam took another step, and Rivan's hand shot out. Vintam yelped as he tripped, falling face-first to the ground. The Silencer's blades flashed before she could even blink. A sword sank into Rivan, and he jerked. Pain and love entwined in his gentle, brown eyes as they found hers, before sinking to the floor, lifeless.

A cry rose in Esta's aching throat.

Her world was gone. Her hope was gone.

Only despair. Only death in the figures pulling her family's murderer to his feet.

Vintam bared his teeth, shoving back his disheveled hair. "Kill—"

Esta turned, stepped to the device, and jammed the iluvan shard into the brackets.

Blinding light erupted from the obelisk, and she stumbled back. Crackling beams of blue raced across its gleaming stone, the hairs on her arms rising as energy flooded the air. The device hummed in her head, and the room shuddered.

"*What have you done?*" Vintam screamed over it.

Esta looked at him and the others, who were staring at the device in horror.

"A scared little girl brought you down. How long do you think the Empire has?"

His face, glazed with terror, was all she saw.

Elowë, keep Jack safe.

Maybe Medin was right. Maybe she'd been put here for a reason, like he and her parents had believed. Even if all she did was set one little boy free, it was reason enough. She loved him, as she had been loved, and he was worth dying for.

The light stuttered, the world quaking as the hum became a roar.

Esta closed her eyes and smiled.

EPILOGUE

Little legs dangled from the back, bouncing with each jolt of the wagon's wheels. Sunlight warmed his bare shins, a breeze blowing through the canvas roof overhead. The small girl behind him whimpered as the wagon bumped over another rock.

"Mama, how much farther?" she whined.

Jack glanced back at the family huddled behind the driver. They weren't very different from him. Commoners. The girl was a bit younger. Her father had tanned, muscled arms, much like the other vineyard workers of Ilagron. The mother, a pretty woman in a faded dress, shushed the girl.

"A little ways, darling. Valleyview is quite a journey."

Jack pushed the shaggy hair from his brow.

Valleyview. He'd never heard of it. Really, he hadn't heard much about anything beyond Ilagron. But he'd picked up enough of the father's conversation with the merchant to know the group was heading for southern Pelnoth. Valleyview was the closest he was likely to get to the border with Orda. Jack might be young, but he knew better than to beg for a ride into enemy lands. That'd only lead to questions. And if he'd learned anything about merchants from his time spying on them at the estate, he knew chances were those near the border likely risked a trip or two farther south for opportunities. Maybe even to Caroca, if the coin was good.

"Are you sure you'll be alright?" the mother asked him, frowning.

It wasn't like the frowns Cook and the other grownups had given him. The woman seemed genuinely concerned. It reminded him of *her*.

"Yeah," said Jack, nodding. "My family lives close to Valleyview."

"But to travel so far alone..."

"Pah, leave the boy be, dear," said the father. "We've seen the troubles in Ilagron. I can't blame a man for sending his son to better fortunes elsewhere, and Pelnoth has them aplenty."

"Aye," added the merchant above them. "And even with its closeness to Orda, I reckon you'll find Valleyview a touch calmer than the happenings behind us."

"Too true." The father shook his head. "Terrible, that ordeal at Giltcrest."

"Aye. I hear the grounds were all torn up. Some kinda explosion. Magic. You can bet your last on it."

"Council lords." The father spat. "They're still trying to figure out who's missing. Not sure who was safe in those gilded halls or caught wandering the fancy gardens."

"Oh, I hear the lot in Agonar are mostly fretting about the wine. I expect it won't be flowing quite as fast for a good while." The merchant chuckled. "Word is there's some big lord of the archon's still missing, too. Right mess for Tibris, it is."

"Hmph," said the father, crossing his arms. "He's probably holed up somewhere nice and comfy. They always are."

Jack turned back to the trees as they wound away behind them. A pair of sparrows darting above the dusty road caught his attention, and he smiled.

"You stopped it, Esta. Just like you said," he whispered. "You set me free from my cage, and I'll make sure everyone, even the king, knows it."

He'd made a promise to a friend. His only friend.

And he wouldn't let her down.

THANK YOU

Thank you for checking out *A Legacy of Ashes*! If you enjoyed the story, would you help me out?

Ratings and reviews are one of the biggest ways you can help indie authors connect with more book lovers. The minute or two you take to add your thoughts on the story (or even just a couple seconds for a rating!) can make all the difference in how the algorithm shares it out

Leave a review!

with more curious readers. It also means the world to me! Pick your favorite place to review (Amazon, Goodreads, etc.), and thanks!

Join my newsletter!

Ready for the next book?

Something new is always on the horizon. Want to know when the next book in *The Oathsworn Chronicles* will arrive? Join other readers on the quest by using the QR code to the left or by going to www.zrmccormick.c om to learn more. My amazing subscribers are always the first to hear the news about Kickstarter, new releases, and freebies.

Still want more?

Don't you hate when a story ends and there are still a dozen more places or things you wish you could explore? Me too. That's why I created a whole page of awesome bonuses for you to dive into while you wait for the next book! From high-resolution maps to

Explore the extras!

short stories to other exclusive content, go to www.zrmccorm ick.com/extras, or scan the QR code to the right to learn more about the world of *The Oathsworn Chronicles*!

ACKNOWLEDGMENTS

Soon after I started the process of publishing the first book in this series, *Awakening*, I knew this story was one I wanted to tell. It wasn't until I ran the Kickstarter campaign for *Awakening*, however, that its chance came. The excitement my Kickstarter backers brought to that crowdfunding campaign is the reason *A Legacy of Ashes* exists today. Backers, without you, I'm not sure when I would've had the chance to tell this story. Thank you for lighting the fire and helping it rise from the dark corners of my ideas and into the light.

Meghan, thank you again for your editing wizardry. Your attention to detail and insight continually push me to refine each story and make it the best it can be. Maybe someday I'll finally nail all those commas and dashes too. (*Although, as Arano would say, it is not a high chance.*)

Rachel, once more you've astounded me with your artistic talents. This book was probably the most challenging I've had to date in terms of ideas to capture the story, but you took those fragments and made them into a coherent design symbolizing its most important elements. Thank you for bringing your ideas and skills to this book.

Ben and Lathem, I can't express all the value you bring to refining my stories as early readers. There are so many little details I rush through on those first drafts, and you don't hesitate to call those out. The criticisms and suggestions you bring challenge me to improve and make each story better for future readers.

Erica, my biggest supporter. How did I get lucky enough to marry someone who not only enjoys my stories, but could've been an editor too? Thank you for being there to bounce ideas off of, to catch my silliest mistakes (before anyone else sees them), and to encourage me to keep going. No matter what, I know I can continue this crazy writing journey because of your love and support. You are such a blessing to me.

For it all, thank you, Jesus. For your love, even when we feel unlovable, caged by our circumstances and choices. You set us free. For those who need hope, let *Ashes* be an extension of your hand, just like Medin's, reaching down to lift someone up and remind them of their true home and the true love that awaits.

THE ALDARIAN COMPENDIUM

If, like the many others before, you've flipped or scrolled to the back of this story because you have no idea what that person just said or where in Aldaria they're at, welcome! Several of the Heraldan Collective's brightest minds have curated this appendix to help you keep everything straight. Within the Compendium, you will find terms listed alphabetically for ease of use. Bear in mind, several scribes continue to work on this ever-expanding tome. Be sure to check back as each new story is discovered!

Addi - a young servant girl of Giltcrest Estate

Agonar - the capital city of Hamidia and the Hamid Empire; the largest city in Edros

Aldaria (ahl-DARE-ee-ah) - the planet and known mortal world

Aljardin (AHL-har-deen) - the provincial capital of Araphon

Alsalaam (AHL-sah-lahm) - a large city in eastern Araphon

Analyn - the deceased wife of Medin

Arano Deshad - a member of the Ashguard; native of Fargost; the greatest swordsman you shall ever meet

Araphon (AIR-ah-fahn) - a large province of the Hamid Empire in northern Edros well known for its vast, uninhabitable desert; most of its cities lie in its grasslands north of the Drag-ontail Mountains or near oases on the desert's edge

Archmage Savos - a powerful nobleman and mage-lord of the Imperial Council; the closest visible advisor to Archon Tibris

Archon Tibris - the ruler of the Hamid Empire

Artis - a member of the Ashguard; native of Hamidia; a powerful mage, particularly skilled in elemental magic

Baron Navan - a nobleman of Hamidia

Braxton - a young servant boy of Giltcrest Estate; bullies Jack and the other children

Brunce - a member of the Ashguard; native of Orda; known for his incredible size and skill in hand-to-hand combat

Captain Thranar - an Imperial officer who led the Hamid Empire's first expedition across the Endless Ocean in 470 GR

Caroca (cah-RAH-cah) - the capital city and a major population center of Orda

Castle Neurim - an important place of governance over the western half of Agonar. Its owner retains a seat on the Imperial Council

Claude - a young servant boy of Giltcrest Estate; bullies Jack and the other children

Comtesse Mirabelle - a noblewoman of Agonar; wife of Count Wilhelm; holds significant influence over other ladies of the Imperial court

Count Hargev -a nobleman and mage-lord of the Imperial Council

Count Wilhelm - a powerful nobleman and mage-lord of the Imperial Council; husband of Comtesse Mirabelle

Davin - the deceased prince of Orda; younger brother of King Attas; husband of Lara

Edros (EH-droas) - also known as the Great Continent; the largest known landmass in Aldaria and birthplace of modern mankind

Elowë (EHL-oh-way) - the Creator, in Elvish; also referred to as the Creator in the modern era; the sole deity and maker of all things known and unknown

Esta - an orphaned street beggar from Orda; works with her brother, Rivan, for the Thieves' Guild to survive

Festival of Triumph - an annual celebration held in Malgavorn to commemorate the Empire's near-unification of Edros; consists of a week-long tournament of contests sponsored by members of the Imperial court, leading up to the Triumphal Ball at the archon's summer palace

Fountmore Academy - a prestigious school in Ilagron; caters to children of nobility and the magically gifted

Ghenda - a Neboan member of the Thieves' Guild operating in Caroca

Giltcrest Estate - a large vineyard and manor outside of Ilagron; owned by Lord Vintam

Glorious Rule (GR) - the naming convention for chronology in the Hamid Empire; events are recorded based on the founding of the Empire and unification of the Hamidian tribes, which began in 0 GR

Hamidia (hah-MID-ee-ah) - the central most nation in Edros; birthplace of the Hamid Empire

High Prince Ibhrar (EEB-rahr) - the highest ruler of the province of Araphon

Ilagron (IHL-aa-grahn) - a large city in southern Hamidia; known for the Fountmore Academy, vineyards, and other agriculture products

Iluvan (ih-LEW-vihn) - silver stone, in Elvish; blue-gray crystals found deep underground containing stores of magical energy

Imperial Council - the governing body of mages overseeing the Hamid Empire; advises the archon in all matters, but is subject to his authority

Imperial Silencers - powerful mages loyal only to the archon; serve as the archon's protectors and secretive agents across Edros

Jack - an orphaned servant boy; raised by the cook of Giltcrest Estate

Karthmoor - a large island nation off the northern coast of Edros

King Attas - the king of Orda

Lady Evie (EE-vee) - a powerful noblewoman and mage of Agonar; wife of Archmage Savos

Lady Katrin - a young noblewoman of Malgavorn

Lady Morven - a young noblewoman of Agonar; wife of Lord Trevan

Lara - the deceased princess of Orda; wife of Davin; sister of Medin; sister-in-law of King Attas

Lord Aragoz - a nobleman and mage-lord of the Imperial Council; rival to Lord Vintam

Lord Gann - an important nobleman of Caroca

Lord Prospen - a nobleman and mage-lord of the Imperial Council; rival to Lord Vintam

Lord Trevan - a nobleman and mage-lord of the Imperial Council; husband of Lady Morven; known for his multiple affairs

Lord Vintam - a powerful nobleman of the Hamid Empire; landowner and winemaker of Ilagron; one of only a few in the Imperial court who does not possess magic

Malgavorn - a large city in central Hamidia; home of the archon's summer palace; hosts the annual Festival of Triumph

Medin (MEH-den) - the Lord of the Ashguard; brother of Lara; relative of King Attas of Orda

Neboa (neh-BOH-ah) - a small nation on the southeastern coast of Edros; unfamiliar to most in the Hamid Empire; known for its tropical climate and unique wildlife

Old Garrow - an elderly street beggar of Caroca

Orda - a large nation of southern Edros; one of only a few to have never been subject to the Hamid Empire

Pelnoth - a small province of the Hamid Empire on the western edge of Edros; an important exporter of seafood and other delicacies

Prince Avaj (AH-vahj) - a merchant prince of Araphon; father of Princess Isla

Princess Isla - a young princess of Araphon; known for her famed beauty; impersonated by Esta to spy on Lord Vintam

Qumrar (koom-RAHR) - a city in southern Araphon

Rivan (RIH-van) - an orphaned street beggar from Orda; works with his sister, Esta, for the Thieves' Guild to survive

Sahar - a small Ordan city near the Shearpoint Mountains

Sand Dragon - enormous, scaled, snakelike creatures native to the Araphon Desert; most nest near the center of the desert

Shearpoint Mountains - a vast, uncharted mountain range in southern Edros; separates the nations of Hamidia, Lynrest, Orda, and Neboa

Sir Perivan - a minor nobleman of Hamidia

Starkhaven - the capital city of Karthmoor; its original settlers are unknown, though it has been the centerpiece of Karthmoor civilization since before the arrival of the Hamid Empire in 250 GR

Steward Gambold - the head steward of Giltcrest Estate

The Ashguard - a secretive spy organization serving the Ordan crown

The Hog Pen - a ramshackle tavern in the slums of Caroca

The Imperial Cult - an ancient religion established by the first archons of the Hamid Empire; worshipped the archon as a godlike ruler; its influence waned during the decades where provinces rebelled and revealed the archon's limited power

Thieves' Guild - a network of thieves and criminals across Edros

Twilight Caves - a vast cave system in the Shearpoint Mountains nearest Orda; known for its beautiful quartz deposits

Valleyview - a small farming village in southeastern Pelnoth on the border with Orda

Vraln - a large coastal city in southern Hamidia

Westrock - a province of the Hamid Empire on the western edge of Edros; primarily composed of dense forests and mountain ranges; a hub of merchants and commerce throughout the continent for centuries

ALSO BY
Z.R. MCCORMICK

The Oathsworn Chronicles

Novels

Book One: Awakening

Novellas

The Cataclysm
A Legacy of Ashes

About the Author

Have you ever imagined exploring another universe?

When Z.R. McCormick outgrew his childhood of cloaks, wooden bows, and plastic swords (which were likely burned to the joy of his neighbors and their landscaping), that wonder inspired by stories of the fantastical was never quite left behind.

He began voyages into the world of Aldaria in between a career in IT, enjoying time with his beautiful wife, and chasing his own rambunctious younglings, culminating in his debut novel, *The Oathsworn Chronicles: Awakening*, released in late 2025. But until that darkness in Aldaria is vanquished, Z.R. is content to read about someone else's adventures with a cold brew and a cozy chair, which, as you might agree, is rather sensible.

Find out more about Z.R. and the world of Aldaria by visiting him at www.zrmccormick.com.

9 781966 180104